# THe TOMOrrOWS' FALL

## Eleanor Devlin

# contents

# Chapter 1

In the bustling city of Chicago in the year 1961, the Tomorrows splendor and affluence reigned high. Their immense wealth, derived mainly from the booming of the oil industry, not only earned them a widespread reputation of prominence and authority but also extended their influence from the political corridors of Washington to the industrial streets of Chicago. Yet, behind this facade of luxury and advantage, lurked a sinister and pernicious force, reminiscent of the insidious seepage of oil through the smallest of cracks.

Carter Tomorrow, the formidable patriarch of the Tomorrow family, stood with a commanding presence in his private study, illuminated by the soft glow of the late afternoon sun. The opulent room was adorned with ornate mahogany bookshelves, rich leather armchairs, and a grand antique desk, adding to the air of old-world sophistication. From his vantage point at the large bay window, his steely gaze was fixed upon the sprawling city skyline, a testament to the Tomorrow family's vast wealth and influence. Yet, despite the beauty before him, a weight of unease sat upon him. The secrets he hid for his wealth where thought to be buried deep, but his doubts of this began to eat at his brain.

"Sir, Mr. Crawford is here to see you," came a faint voice from the doorway.

Carter turned slowly to face Martin, his loyal butler for twenty years. "Send him in," he said, his voice gravelly with exhaustion.

In walked James Crawford, the family lawyer, his polished briefcase and sharp suit making a striking impression. Yet, a tension in his eyes mirrored Carter's own. The two had been close since Carter took the helm at Tomorrow Oil, but their once strong bond was beginning to fracture under the weight of the secrets that crept behind the company and family's new approach to business.

"James," Carter greeted him stiffly, gesturing to the leather chair across from his desk. "I assume you've come with an update."

Crawford nodded, sitting down but not relaxing. "I've got the paperwork. The deed for the offshore rigs in Venezuela. They have been finalized. But, Carter..." His voice trailed off, as tried to choose his next words carefully.

"But what?" Carter's voice cut through the silent air.

"There are rumors. Whispers from Washington. People are asking questions about the labor practices at the rigs. Exploitation, safety violations... If this gets out, it could destroy the whole operation."

Carter's expression didn't change, but his fingers curled tightly around the armrest. The rumors had been buzzing under the surface for years, but as long as the oil production continued, he had believed they would never become more than whispers. Now, he wasn't so sure.

"I'll handle it," Carter said after a pause, his tone steady. "I always do."

Crawford shifted uneasily. "And what about your family? They can't know about this."

Carter's eyes darkened. He thought of his wife, Evelyn, with her grace and glamour who had been the perfect image of a socialite—except she wasn't as oblivious as she seemed. Then there were his children. Samuel, the eldest, was already being prepped to take over Tomorrow Oil, but his ambitions were too reckless, too eager to forge his own legacy, even if it meant leaving his father's empire in shambles. Then there was Celeste, the golden daughter, who flirted too closely with scandal in her search for excitement that wealth couldn't buy.

"I'll take care of my them. You just keep this contained." Carter's words were firm.

James nodded, though his worry lingered. As he collected his papers and left the room, Carter remained standing, the weight of the issues at hand pressed on him like the gravity of the oil that had made him wealthy. He lit a cigarette and stared out into the distance, his thoughts consumed by the storm he could feel coming to his doorstep.

Across the house, Evelyn Tomorrow sat in her parlor, the sunlight beaming in through the French doors, illuminating the fine china tea set before her. She smiled politely at her guest, Sylvia Daugherty, the wife of a prominent senator. The two women had been engaged in deep gossip for the past hour, trading harmless tidbits about the latest whispers in their world. But Evelyn's mind was elsewhere, swirling with thoughts she could never let on that she knew.

She had found something that could put her danger if she let on that she knew.

The night before, while searching for one of Carter's cufflinks in his study, she had stumbled across a folder. A name had been written on the front—Charlotte Rivers. The same Charlotte who had mysteriously vanished five years ago after working as Carter's father's secretary. It had been assumed she had moved away for a fresh start, but Evelyn had her doubts. Finding Charlotte's name again, after all these years, left a knot in her stomach.

Evelyn's hand trembled slightly as she poured another cup of tea, careful not to let her guest see her discomfort. Whatever Carter was hiding, it went deeper than business. And if the past was coming back to bite him, it would take all of Evelyn's wits and charm to keep their family from crumbling.

Upstairs, Samuel sat at his desk, poring over the financial documents. He was no stranger to the company's shady dealings, but he had his own plans to take it in a new direction. His father's reign was growing tired, weak. Samuel wanted to modernize the business, to break free of the old world constraints Carter clung to so firmly. But he wasn't aware of danger that came with it. He knew there were secrets buried deep within the foundation of Tomorrow Oil—secrets that could either make or break his future. And he was willing to do whatever it took to be the one holding the cards in the end.

Meanwhile, Celeste Tomorrow was nowhere near the mansion. Instead, she was speeding down Lake Shore Drive in a red convertible, her laughter mingling with the roar of the engine. At twenty-one, Celeste was the embodiment of youthful rebellion, and her parents' wealth had given her a firm safety net that she constantly tested. With her golden hair flying in the wind and dark sunglasses masking her eyes, Celeste didn't care about the gala she was supposed to attend or the whispers that swirled around her wherever she went.

She was living life on the edge, teetering between society's expectations and her own strive for freedom. Tonight, she was meeting an artist in a forgotten corner of the city—someone who saw her not as the spoiled daughter of a powerful family but as someone real. Someone dangerous. Celeste thrived on the risk, the thrill of being with someone her family would never approve of. But even as she flirted with scandal, there was a restlessness inside her that no amount of rebellion could contain.

As the sun began to set over the city, casting long shadows across the mansion, each member of the Tomorrow family was alone in their private corners of the house—or far beyond it—yet they were all connected by the same tangled web of lies and ambition. The facade of perfection that surrounded them was beginning to show its cracks, and beneath it, something sinister was beginning to brew.

None of them knew just how close they were to the danger that was coming, All their secrets were coming out, and no one. was safe.

# CHAPTER 2

The grand ballroom of the Tomorrow mansion sparkled beneath the chandeliers, each light casting a golden glow over the guests. It was a night of high society, an event where business deals were discussed over champagne flutes, and alliances were formed with a simple handshake. The Tomorrow family's annual gala was the talk of the city, and tonight, every influential figure in Chicago was in attendance, dressed in their best, each vying for a moment with Carter Tomorrow.

Evelyn Tomorrow moved effortlessly through the crowd, her smile as polished as the pearls around her neck. She exchanged pleasantries, managing the guests with an ease that belied the storm of thoughts swirling behind her eyes. Carter stood near the center of the room, flanked by business associates, his sharp gaze sweeping the room, while Samuel worked the edges, shaking hands and making connections. He was his father's shadow for tonight, watching, waiting, and calculating.

But as height of the evening approached, the absence of Celeste became more apparent.

"Where is Celeste?" Evelyn scolded to Carter, her voice low, but her words laced with frustration. "She was supposed to be here by now."

Carter glanced at her, his jaw tightening. "She'll show. She always does, you know she likes to make an entrance." But even as he spoke, there was a flicker of doubt. Celeste's reckless behavior had always been a thorn in his side, a constant reminder that some things—even his own family—were beyond his control.

Meanwhile, miles away from the glittering ballroom, Celeste was not concerned with society's or her family's expectations. She had abandoned the thought of the gala hours earlier, speeding through the heart of the city with a sense of freedom. The wind in her hair, the distant hum of Lake Michigan, the glow of lights in the city beamed passed her—all of it made her feel alive in a way that the sterile elegance of her family's gala never could.

She pulled up to a small, run-down warehouse in one of Chicago's forgotten industrial districts. It was a world away from the pristine streets she grew up on. The warehouse was the makeshift studio of Victor Armand, a brooding, enigmatic painter Celeste had been interested in for months. He wasn't like the suitors her family paraded before her—he was dark, dangerous, and completely indifferent to her wealth.

She found him intoxicating.

Victor had told her he would paint her tonight, capture her spirit in a way no one else ever could. She imagined the final product hanging in some forgotten gallery, a defiant testament to her rebellion. She stepped inside, the air was chilly with the scent of paint and cigarettes.

"Victor?" Celeste called, her voice echoing in the cavernous space.

He appeared from the shadows, his eyes darker than she remembered. His usual smirk was gone, replaced with something harder, colder.

"You came," he said, but there was no warmth in his voice.

"Of course I did," she replied, stepping closer, her excitement growing. "Are you ready to paint me?"

Victor's gaze followed her movements, but something in the air had changed. Before Celeste could react, a sharp, sudden pain struck the back of her head. Her vision blurred, the world spinning as she stumbled forward. The last thing she saw before the darkness took her was Victor's expression—calm, calculating, and completely devoid of the passion that once drew her to him.

Back at the gala, the night was winding down. Carter stood at the edge of the room, speaking in hushed tones with a senator about a potential oil deal overseas. Samuel hovered nearby, occasionally stepping into conversations to assert his presence, but his eyes frequently glared toward the entrance. He had expected Celeste to show by now, her usual dramatic flair timed perfectly to cause a scene, but there was no sign of her.

Evelyn, too, had begun to notice. She excused herself from her conversation and slipped out into the hallway, retrieving to the kitchen to check with the staff. After a few quiet words, her brows furrowed. No one had seen Celeste all night.

As she reentered the ballroom, she found Samuel waiting for her, his expression concerned. "Mother, where is she?"

"I haven't a clue," Evelyn whispered, her composure cracking slightly. "This isn't like her. She would have made her grand entrance by now."

Just as she spoke, Carter approached, his eyes narrowing as he sensed the tension between them. "What's going on?"

"It's Celeste," Samuel said quietly. "She hasn't been at home all day. No one has seen her."

Carter's face hardened instantly. He motioned for them to follow him into a side room, away from the curious eyes and ears of the guests. Once they were alone, Carter's voice dropped to a low, dangerous growl. "What do you mean? Where is she?"

Evelyn shook her head. "We don't know. She hasn't been seen all night."

Before anyone could respond, the house phone rang. Samuel answered, expecting it to be a servant with an update, but the voice on the other end was not what he expected.

"Listen carefully," came a rough voice, distorted as though through a cheap filter. "We have your daughter."

Samuel's grip tightened on the receiver. "Who is this?" he demanded, his voice low but urgent.

I may be a mystery to you, but your father holds all the answers. The important thing is that Celeste... is with me, and if you want her back, you'll follow my instructions."

Carter grabbed the phone from Samuel's hand, his expression murderous. "What the hell do you want?"

The voice on the other end paused for a beat as if savoring the moment. "Two million dollars. In cash. And no police or your daughter disappears for good."

Carter's face went pale with rage, but his voice was steady. "You'll get your money. But if anything happens to her, I'll find you, and I'll make sure you regret ever laying a hand on my daughter."

The line went dead.

Evelyn gasped, her hand flying to her mouth, her mask of composure crumbling as the reality set in. "Who would do this? Who would take her?"

Carter's eyes were cold, his mind already racing through possibilities. He had enemies—people who wanted to see him brought down, competitors, rivals. But the ruthlessness of this move was unexpected, even for them.

"It doesn't matter," Carter said grimly. "We'll get her back. No one threatens my family and gets away with it."

Celeste regained consciousness in the dim, eerie light of the warehouse, feeling a sharp throbbing in her head and discovering that her wrists were tightly bound behind her back. A surge of panic shot through her as she pieced together what had transpired. She strained against the restraints, her breath becoming rapid and shallow as fear consumed her. In.

Victor loomed over her, his eyes once filled with warmth now glinting with icy indifference. "You were always too trusting," he murmured softly, his voice devoid of the tenderness that had once ensnared her heart.

"Why?" Celeste's voice was hoarse, her throat dry.

"It was never about you," he replied, turning away from her. "It's about your father. And now, we wait."

Celeste could feel her heart pounding like a drum inside her chest, sending tremors through her entire body. Her mind was in a whirlwind of fear and confusion, a storm of emotions that threatened to overwhelm her. She had always prided herself on her ability to remain in control, but now, she felt utterly trapped and helpless, like a pawn in a dangerous game she couldn't even begin to comprehend.

# CHAPTER 3

The opulence of the Tomorrow mansion felt suffocating in the wake of the kidnapper's call. The grand ballroom, which had been filled with music and laughter just hours earlier, was now silent and cold. Every tick of the grandfather clock in the hallway echoed like a gunshot, counting down the seconds until they would receive more instructions.

Carter sat at his desk in the study, the same desk where he had conducted countless business deals that had made him wealthy beyond measure. But this was different. This wasn't business. This was his daughter's life hanging in the balance.

The demand had been explicitly stated: two million dollars in cash, no involvement of law enforcement, and no attempts at deception. However, Carter was acutely aware that even if they adhered to the kidnappers' instructions flawlessly, this situation was far from straightforward. Guarantee that Celeste would be returned unscathed. He had dealt with dangerous people before. He had seen what desperation and greed could drive someone to do. And if the people who had taken Celeste were as ruthless as they seemed, they could do anything.

Evelyn sat across from him, her hands trembling, clutching the fabric of her silk dress as though holding onto it could keep her from falling apart. Her eyes were bloodshot, and the grace and beauty she carried with her now cracked like glass.

"Why her?" she whispered, her voice breaking. "Why our daughter?"

Carter's eyes blazed with intensity, his jaw locked tight. "It's not about her. It's about me. This is retaliation. Someone's out to get me."

The realization sent a chill down Evelyn's spine. "But... but this is Celeste! How could anyone be so cruel, so heartless as to hurt her?"

Enemies are a part of my life," Carter said with a grim tone. "I've made deals and done things that have earned me some powerful adversaries. Stepped on people to get where we are. This was bound to happen sooner or later."

Evelyn's eyes widened in a mix of fear and revulsion as she recoiled. "You always said everything you did was for the family. You..." promised us we were safe!"

"I did what I had to do," Carter said coldly, standing up from his chair, his hands tightening into fists. "I built this empire for us. But I can't control what people do when they want revenge."

Evelyn looked away, her breath catching in her throat. She had always known Carter's business dealings were more than just ruthless—they were dangerous. But this? Is their daughter being kidnapped and held for ransom? This was a nightmare she hadn't prepared for.

Samuel paced furiously in the hall outside his father's study, his mind racing. His sister was missing, held hostage by people they didn't know, and they were being blackmailed like some common criminals. It infuriated him.

He slammed his fist against the wall, frustration and fear coursing through him. How could this have happened? He had spent years positioning himself to take over the family empire, to be the one in control. Now, control had been ripped away from him, and it wasn't his business at stake—it was Celeste's life.

He couldn't help but think about her, his little sister who constantly pushed the limits and seemed to thrive on danger. Despite finding her antics exhausting, she was still his blood. And... despite their differences, he would do anything to get her back.

"We need to hit them where it hurts," Samuel muttered under his breath, his mind spinning with dangerous thoughts. "If we give them the money, they'll think we're weak. We need to track them down and crush them. Make them regret ever touching her."

He envisioned leveraging every available resource—private investigators, mercenaries, anyone unafraid to do what it takes. He'd compensate them handsomely to track down the kidnappers and put an end to this once and for all. But as much as he yearned to take action, Samuel understood that recklessness would jeopardize Celeste's life even further. At present, he had to bide his time and go along with the plan, but just the idea made him queasy.

Evelyn, too, was coming undone, but in a different way. She retreated to her room, where she closed the door and collapsed onto the bed, sobbing. The weight of her helplessness crushed her chest. She had always been the composed one, the one who kept the family together with her grace and calm. But now, she felt like she was unraveling from the inside out.

She had no idea where her daughter was or what condition she was in. Was she scared? Was she hurt? The questions circled relentlessly in her mind, each one darker than the last.

A sudden thought pierced through her panic. What if Carter had known this was coming? What if he had made another one of his secret deals, and Celeste was paying the price? The doubts gnawed at her, feeding her fears. She had found the document with Charlotte Rivers' name, and now this. What else had Carter done in the shadows?

She needed answers. But for now, all she could do was cling to the hope that they would hear from the kidnappers again—and that they would be merciful.

The next morning, as the sun barely crept over the horizon, a second phone call came. The sound of the phone ringing sent a jolt of panic through the mansion. Carter snatched it up immediately, his heart pounding in his chest.

"Do you have my money?" the distorted voice asked, calm and in control.

"Yes," Carter replied, his voice tense. "We have the money. Just tell me where to drop it."

There was a pause. "Good. You'll receive instructions shortly. Remember—no police. If I get even a hint of interference, your daughter will pay the price."

The line went dead.

Carter placed the phone down, his hands trembling for the first time in years. He turned to Samuel and Evelyn, who stood anxiously in the doorway. "They're sending instructions," he said flatly.

"We should have police on standby," Samuel said, his voice cold and determined. "If we can track them, we can strike the moment Celeste is safe."

"No," Carter barked. "They said no police. They'll kill her if they even suspect we've gone against their demands."

"We're just going to sit here and wait, then?" Samuel's eyes burned with frustration. "We're letting them have all the power, while Celeste's life hangs in the balance?"

Carter said nothing for a moment, staring at his son. "I won't risk her life, Samuel. Not for pride, not for control. When it comes to family, you make the sacrifices."

Samuel clenched his fists but said nothing further, the weight of his father's words settling heavily between them.

Hours later, a plain brown envelope arrived at the mansion, slipped through the gate by an unknown courier. Inside were the instructions: a remote location on the outskirts of the city where the money was to be delivered, and a chilling warning that no one was to follow. Any deviation and Celeste would die.

The tension in the house was unbearable. Carter, Evelyn, and Samuel gathered in the study, the envelope lying open on the desk. Each of them was holding onto their fear in their way, but the pressure was mounting.

Carter's thoughts drifted to the deal he had made with an arms dealer years ago, deal that had gone south and ruined a man's life. Could this be payback? Could this be connected? He didn't know, and the uncertainty was gnawing at him. But one thing was clear: someone wanted to make him bleed, and they were using his daughter to do it.

As the evening approached, the tension thickened, and the mansion felt like a tomb. Time was slipping through their fingers, and with each passing hour, the chances of seeing Celeste alive seemed to dwindle.

And as the night descended, the Tomorrow family prepared to face the most dangerous crossroads of their lives, each willing to sacrifice whatever it took to save Celeste—except none of them knew just how far that price would go.

# CHAPTER 4

The night surrounded them in suffocating darkness, a tense calm before the storm. The Tomorrows were ready to act, and Carter had reached his breaking point. He refused to bow down to Victor. He now knew what he had feared. That arms deal had come back to bite him. Victor was an associate of that dealer who got screwed over.

In the study's dim light, Carter and Samuel stood side by side. Samuel pulled on black gloves, his face reflecting fierce resolve. Despite their rehearsed plan, an undercurrent of doubt pulsed through Carter. Revenge may not be elegant, but it was their only option.

Carter whispered confidently, fixing his gaze on the intricate map of Victor Reynard's secretive hideout. Reynard, the notorious artist who had abducted Celeste for a hefty ransom, was not just another criminal. He was cunning, shrewd, and backed by dangerous allies. But Carter possessed what Reynard lacked: the means, the alliances, and the unyielding determination to crush anyone who dared challenge his dominion.

Samuel's eyes narrowed as he looked at the map. "We're sure this is where he's holding her?"

"Positive," Carter said, his voice a low growl. "Our contact inside Reynard's operation confirmed it this morning. This is where he's hiding her—and this is where we'll strike."

Samuel glanced up at his father, his jaw clenched. "And what about the money? Are we still delivering the ransom?"

"We'll bring the money," Carter said, his voice hardening. "But we're not leaving without making Reynard pay for what he's done. When we have Celeste, we burn his operation to the ground."

Samuel nodded, his face set in stone. The Tomorrows had never been a family that took well to threats, and this was no different. The plan was simple—lure Reynard into thinking he had the upper hand with the ransom drop, then strike. And they would hit him where it hurt: his illicit empire. For a man like Reynard, money and power were everything, and taking that from him would be the deepest cut of all.

As Carter turned to leave the study, Evelyn appeared at the doorway, her face pale but resolute. "You're sure this is the only way?"

"There's no other choice," Carter said, meeting her gaze. "We can't negotiate with people like Reynard. If we do, it'll never stop."

Evelyn nodded, though the unease still flickered in her eyes. "Just... bring her back. No matter what it takes."

Carter's hand tightened into a fist. "I will."

In the dimly lit remote warehouse, Celeste was tied to a chair, the ropes were digging into her wrists, leaving them raw and bloody. The hours in captivity seemed to drag on endlessly, distorting into a seemingly slow passage of time. Her disorientation was compounded by the absence of her watch, leaving her feeling both mentally and physically strained as if each passing moment stretched into what felt like eternity.

Reynard had come to see her twice—the first time to demand the ransom, and the second time to emphasize the consequences of not meeting his demand. His words lingered in her mind, oozing with malice.

"Do you believe your father is untouchable?" Reynard taunted, a sinister smirk playing on his lips. "We both know he's not. His enemies are lurking everywhere. And now, you're going to assist me in bringing him down."

At first, she resisted, telling him she would never betray her family, but the isolation was wearing her down. She could feel the walls closing in, and the fear that pulsed through her veins grew stronger with each passing moment. What if the money didn't come? What if her father couldn't save her?

And then, Reynard had made her an offer.

"Help me expose your father's dirty secrets," he had said, leaning in close, "and I'll let you go. You can walk away from this with your life. I know everything about Tomorrow Oil—the illegal labor, the payoffs, the disappearances. You know the truth too, don't you, Celeste? I've seen the way you look at him. He's not the hero you think he is."

She had stayed silent at first, refusing to give him the satisfaction of seeing her doubt. But the seed had been planted, and now, as she sat alone in the darkness, it began to take root.

Her father wasn't a hero. He was ruthless, calculating, and dangerous. She had seen it in the way he ran their family, the way he controlled their lives. He had built an empire, yes, but at what cost? And for what? Power? Money? Was it worth it if she was the one who had to pay for it?

The door creaked open, and Reynard stepped into the room, his silhouette dark against the dim light. "Have you thought about my offer?" he asked casually, as though they were discussing a business deal.

Celeste gazed at him, her heart pounding. This was her moment. Her opportunity to break free from her father's grasp and to take her rightful place as the heir of the company over her brother.

"I've made up my mind," she declared firmly, her voice steady.

Reynard arched an eyebrow, intrigued. "And?"

"I will work with you," she stated, the words tasting bitter on her tongue. "But only if you guarantee my freedom."

Reynard's smile grew, but his eyes remained icy. "You have my word."

Celeste felt a lump form in her throat as she considered the difficult situation. She knew that going against her father would have serious repercussions, but she thought it would be worth the risk.

Back in the heart of Chicago, the Tomorrows were gearing up for action. Carter had sent out his top men with one mission: retrieve Celeste and dismantle every part of Reynard's operation. It was about to go down, and nothing would stand in their way.

The clock struck midnight at the desolate, abandoned warehouse on the edge of the city. This was no ordinary meeting place—it was a hotspot for low-profile transactions and shady deals orchestrated by men like Carter. However, tonight was different. What was supposed to be just another deal turned into a deadly ambush.

As Carter and Samuel pulled up to the warehouse in a sleek black car, the tension was thick. Carter's heart pounded in his chest, though he showed no sign of it. His thoughts were solely on his daughter and how he would tear Reynard apart for taking her.

"Are you ready?" Carter asked Samuel as they stepped out of the car, the night air cool and biting.

Samuel nodded, his face set in grim determination. "Let's finish this."

They approached the warehouse, carrying the briefcase filled with the ransom money. Carter had brought it as a show of good faith, but he had never intended of handing it over. This was the bait, and Reynard was about to walk right into their trap.

In the depths of the warehouse, Reynard bided his time, his men covered in the darkness. Meanwhile, Celeste, restrained and silenced, observed the unfolding events with a blend of fear and excitement. Having committed to her decision, she now questioned herself as her father and brother ventured into the warehouse.

The tension broke when Reynard appeared from the darkness, his smile gleaming like a predator. "You have the money?"

"I have it," Carter said coldly. "But I want my daughter first."

Reynard laughed, the sound low and menacing. "Oh, you'll get her back, Mr. Tomorrow. But not before I get what I want."

The next moments were a blur. Carter gave the signal, and his men moved in from the shadows, guns drawn. A firefight erupted, chaos filling the warehouse as bullets flew with men shouting. Samuel grabbed Celeste, cutting her bindings as they made a run for the exit.

Reynard, witnessing his empire crumble before his very eyes, turned to Celeste, his face contorted in rage. "You promised to help me!"

"Farewell, Victor," she whispered.

Carter's men closed in, and as the dust settled, Reynard was left in ruins—his empire destroyed, his revenge turned to ashes. The relentless pursuit had finally come to a spectacular end, setting the stage for an epic showdown that would be remembered.

The Tomorrows were relieved to have their daughter back, but as they drove away from the burning wreckage of Reynard's operation, a new tension was brewing beneath the surface. Celeste hadn't shared the deal she had made with Reynard, and as they pulled into the driveway of their mansion, she wondered just how much longer she could keep it hidden.

For now, the Tomorrows had won. But in their world, a victory always came with a cost.

# CHAPTER 5

The sun hung low in the sky, casting a dim, glow over the Tomorrow estate. Inside, Celeste stood at her bedroom window, her reflection staring back at her through the glass. She looked tired—wiser somehow, though it had only been days since her return. The relief of her rescue had been quickly replaced by a heaviness that pressed down on her chest with her every breath.

Victor Reynard was supposed to be dead. Her father and Samuel had made sure of it. They had set fire to his warehouse, burning it down with a level of ruthlessness that was sure to end him. Carter had been so proud, when the flames swallowed the evidence of their crimes, confident that they had eliminated the man who dared to take what was his.

But Celeste knew better.

Victor was very much alive. And he had made her an offer she couldn't refuse.

At first, it had been about survival—a desperate attempt to make it out. But now, standing in the aftermath of it all, she realized her deal with Victor was much more complicated. It was an opportunity. An opportunity to seize control, to shape the future of the family empire the way she wanted it.

Power, that once felt impossible was in her grasp.

Celeste smoothed a hand over her blouse and turned from the window. She had seen how her father looked at her since her return—how he showered her with affection, praised her for her strength, never once suspecting the her sinister intentions lurking beneath her smile. And that was his weakness. He couldn't see her for what she really was because he was blind by his love for her.

But love was a weakness. And she would not make that mistake for anyone.

In the parlor downstairs, Evelyn sat in her usual spot, the fine china tea set before her untouched. She had been replaying the events of Celeste's capture in her mind, trying to make sense of the uneasy feeling that she had in her gut. Something wasn't right. Her daughter had always been headstrong and resilient, but there was something different about her now—something cold and calculating.

She took a small sip of tea, her eyes narrowing as she thought back to when they brought Celeste home. Her daughter had seemed shaken, of course, but the fear had faded too quickly. Almost as if she had expected it to. And when Carter had pulled her into his arms, whispering promises of safety, Evelyn had seen the flicker of something in Celeste's eyes—something she hadn't liked.

"Mother."

Evelyn startled, looking up to see Celeste standing in the doorway, her expression unreadable.

"I didn't mean to startle you," Celeste said innocently, stepping into the room.

Evelyn smiled, though it didn't reach her eyes. "You didn't. Come, sit with me."

Celeste crossed the room and sat down beside her mother, the air between them thick with unspoken words. Evelyn studied her daughter for a long moment, taking in the subtle difference in her demeanor—the way Celeste carried herself now, with more confidence, more purpose.

"How are you feeling?" Evelyn asked curiously, her voice laced with concern.

"I'm fine, Mother," Celeste replied, a small, practiced smile playing on her lips. "I'm just glad to be back home."

Evelyn nodded, but the feeling of unease only deepened. "You've been through so much. You can talk to me, you know. About anything."

Celeste's smiled faltered, just for a second, but she quickly recovered. "I know. But I'm fine now. Really."

Evelyn watched her daughter closely, her instincts telling her that something was up with her. But before she could press further, Celeste stood up, smoothing out her skirt.

"I think I'll take a walk," she said, her tone light, but there was a sharp edge to her voice that Evelyn didn't miss.

As Celeste left the room, Evelyn's eyes followed her, a deep suspicion settling in her chest. Something had changed in her daughter. And Evelyn was determined to find out what.

Across the house, Samuel sat at his desk, papers strewn across the surface as he tried to focus on his task. But his mind kept drifting back to his sister. Since her return, he had noticed the subtle shift in her demeanor, the way she carried herself with more purpose, more control. It didn't sit right with him.

Growing up, Celeste had always been the golden child—the one who was able to charm anyone, the one who could do nothing wrong. But Samuel knew her better than anyone. He knew her ambition, her hunger for more. And now, after the kidnapping, that hunger had only grown. He had seen it in her eyes.

Something had happened while she was with Reynard, something that had changed her. And Samuel wasn't sure he liked what he was seeing.

He leaned back in his chair, running a hand through his hair as the thought gnawed at him. Celeste had always been cunning, but this felt different—more alarming. She wasn't just playing the game anymore; she was trying to win it. And if she was after the family business, Samuel knew she would stop at nothing.

His thoughts were interrupted by the sound of footsteps in the hallway, and he looked up just as his sister passed by his door. For a moment, their eyes met, and in that brief exchange, Samuel felt a chill run down his spine.

Celeste smiled at him, but there was something cold in her gaze—something serious.

And in that moment, Samuel realized the truth.

She was coming for his spot as the heir of the company.

Later that evening, as the family gathered for dinner, the tension was noticable. Carter, oblivious to the undercurrents swirling around him, sat at the head of the table, smiling proudly at his postcard daughter. He had been attached to her hip ever since her return, blinded by his love for her, unable to see the darkness that had begun to grow inside her.

"Celeste," he said, his voice warm, "I've been thinking. Perhaps it's time we bring you into the business more. You've always been sharp, and after everything that's happened, I think it's only fitting that you take on a more creative and active role."

Evelyn glanced up quickly, her fork paused mid-air. Samuel's jaw tightened, but he said nothing, his eyes fixed on Celeste.

Celeste looked up, her expression carefully composed. "I'd like that, Father. I've been thinking a lot about that to... and I would be honored to be more involved."

Carter beamed, completely unaware of the tension in the room. "Good. We'll start tomorrow. There's a lot you can learn, and I want you right by my side."

Celeste smiled sweetly, but beneath the surface, her mind was racing. This was the opportunity she needed.. The business, the power, the legacy—it was all within her reach now. All she had to do was play her cards well.

And if that meant selling out the family secrets to get there, then so be it.

As the night continued on, the family dispersed, each retreating to their own corners of the mansion. But the tension and unease lingered, thick and suffocating. Evelyn watched her daughter closely, her suspicions growing with every passing moment. Samuel, too, kept his distance, his eyes close on Celeste.

And Celeste? She walked through the halls of the Tomorrow mansion, a smile on her lips and a plan in her heart.

She would take everything. And she wouldn't stop until the Tomorrow name was hers alone.

Her footsteps echoed through the empty hallway, the house falling into a quiet, unsettling calm. Celeste entered her bedroom and closed the door behind her. As she reached for the lamp on her bedside table, the phone rang.

She froze.

There were only a few people who would call her this late, and most of them were downstairs or asleep.

Slowly, she picked up the receiver. "Hello?"

A familiar voice, smooth and low, oozed through the line. "Miss Tomorrow, I trust your family still thinks I'm dead?"

Celeste's breath caught in her throat. Victor Reynard.

"They do," she whispered, her heart racing. "But you need to stay that way for now. If they find out you're alive—"

"I'm not worried about your father, Celeste," Victor interrupted, his voice dripping with confidence. "We both know he's blinded when it comes to you. What I'm concerned with is whether you're still committed to our arangemnt."

Celeste's fingers tightened around the receiver. The deal they had made—the secrets she had promised in exchange for her life—was still hanging over her.

"I'm committed," she said, her voice steady despite the uneasy feeling swirling inside her. "But this needs to be handled carefully."

Victor chuckled darkly. "Careful is my specialty. Just remember, Celeste, you owe me. And when the time comes, you'll deliver."

The line went dead before she could respond, leaving Celeste standing in the darkness, her pulse pounding in her ears. She had made her choice. She had sold her loyalty to Victor Reynard, and now there was no going back.

If she wanted to take over the Tomorrow empire, she would have to pay the ultimate price. The cost would be her family.

# CHAPTER 6

The crisp autumn air surrounded the Tomorrow estate, the scent of decaying leaves and wood smoke hanging in the air as Evelyn Tomorrow sat by the grand piano in the parlor. Her slender fingers traced the ivory keys absent-mindedly, her mind far from the music and  the safety of the sprawling mansion. She had been restless for days now, haunted by a secret only she and one other person should have ever known. But Evelyn felt eyes on her—judgmental, prying eyes from within her own home.

Celeste.

Since her daughter's return, Evelyn had sensed something was brewing, but Carter had brushed off her concerns as mere paranoia. Celeste was back to her old self, he'd said. But Evelyn knew better. She could feel the change in the air, and it wasn't just the coming winter. Celeste was colder, more daring, her once-vibrant eyes now gleaming with som ething... reckless.

The sound of approaching footsteps caused Evelyn to stiffen. She turned, the weight of a thousand fears suddenly settling onto her chest as Celeste entered the room.

"Mother." Celeste's voice was smooth, unsettlingly calm. "We have to talk."

Evelyn forced a smile, trying to hide the unease that twisted on the inside of her. "Of course, dear. What is it?"

Celeste didn't sit. She stood, a statue of poised control, her eyes fixed on her mother with such an intensity that made Evelyn's pulse race. "I know about Charlotte."

The words were like a gunshot in the silence.

Evelyn's fingers froze above the keys, her blood running cold. "What are you talking about?" she said, her voice barely a whisper. She tried to keep her composure, but the panic was setting in, clawing at her.

"You know exactly what I'm talking about, Mother." Celeste's lips curved into a smile that held no warmth. "Father's old assistant. The one you sent away."

Evelyn's breath hitched. "Celeste, you don't understand. That was years ago, and it's not—"

"It's not relevant anymore?" Celeste interrupted, her tone mocking. "It's not important because it was 'handled'? Do you really think that things like this just disappear? That they fade into the past without a trace?" Her eyes gleamed with something dark. "Or did you think I wouldn't find out?"

Evelyn stood, her body trembling. "Celeste, please, I did what I had to for this family. For your father. For brother and for you."

"Don't insult me." Celeste's voice was ice. "This isn't about what you did for us. It's about what you did for yourself. Charlotte was a loose end that threatened your perfect world, so you buried silenced her."

The accusation hung heavy between them, each word sinking into Evelyn's chest like a weight. She had always known this moment would come—feared it—but never imagined it would be her daughter standing on the other side, delivering the fatal blow.

"What do you want from me?" Evelyn asked, her voice breaking, tears threatening to fall.

Celeste took a step forward, her expression softening just enough to make Evelyn feel the trap tightening around her. "It's simple, Mother. You're going to help me. You're going to do exactly what I need to do, or I will make sure Father, Samuel, and the entire world know exactly why you sent to Charlotte away and all abut the affair and pregnancy."

Evelyn felt her knees buckle. "Celeste, you wouldn't dare. This is your family. You can't destroy it like this."

Celeste tilted her head, her eyes narrowing. "You think I'm trying to destroy this family? No, Mother. I'm going to save it. But to do that, I need control. I need to make sure everyone falls in line. And you, dear Mother, are going to be the first."

Evelyn's heart pounded in her chest, her mind reeling. "What more do you want?"

"I want you to start with Father," Celeste said simply. "You're going to help me convince him to let me in, to let me sit in and observe. Let's face it, Samuel doesn't have the heart or the sack to take on all of this. He would crumble under the pressure and you know it. You are going to help me convince father that I should be his right chair."

"And if I refuse?" Evelyn asked, her voice small, broken.

Celeste smiled again, that same cold, cruel smile. "Then Charlotte and father's affair will no longer be kept hidden. And Mother, believe me, that will only be the beginning. You're not the only one in this house with skeletons in the closet. I know them all now. Every last one. I am prepared to do whatever it takes at any cost."

Evelyn could feel the world closing in around her, the walls of her perfectly manicured life crumbling right before her eyes. This was her daughter, her flesh and blood, and yet... she had never felt so utterly helpless.

"I... I'll do it," Evelyn whispered, the fight draining out of her. "Just remember though. If you go too far and start to sink I won't save you.'

Celeste nodded, satisfied. "Good. We'll talk again soon, Mother." She turned to leave but paused at the doorway, looking back over her shoulder. "And remember, I don't need you. You need me let me make that clear."

Evelyn collapsed onto the piano bench as Celeste disappeared into the hallway, her body shaking with silent sobs. She had always known the Tomorrow family had deadly secrets, but she had never imagined that her own daughter would be the one to use them to take advantage of her.

And now, the blackmail had begun.

Celeste was in control or so she thought. Samuel was on hot on her trail and she knew it. But, she had a trick up her sleeve for him and would play the card when he made the first move.

She had everyone's secrets in her back pocket and when the time was right they all had to play her rules. Even Victor she had things on him and she knew that when the time came that she would have to use it.

This was all on her time and she knew her mother wouldn't dare try to cross her.

# CHAPTER 7

The sun hung low in the sky, casting long shadows over the Tomorrow estate. From the outside, everything appeared as it always had—grand, unshakable. But inside the mansion, there was a storm coming, one that had already begun to tear at the very fabric of the family.

Evelyn Tomorrow sat in her bedroom, her mind wandering with the conversation she'd just had with Celeste. Her daughter had come back a different person—troubled, determined—but if Celeste thought she could hold Evelyn captive with one secret, she was more foolish than Evelyn had realized. After all, the Tomorrow family had always thrived on secrets. Blackmail was nothing Evelyn hadn't experienced before and far more scary people then her daughter.

She glanced at the clock. Samuel would be home soon, and she had only a narrow window to set things in motion before Celeste realized what was happening. Evelyn stood, smoothing down her dress, and moved swiftly toward the grand library where Samuel often retreated after long days of overseeing the business. He was sharp, perhaps sharper than his father, and Evelyn knew she could count on him to play his part.

As she entered the library, she found Samuel at the large oak desk, poring over financial documents, his brow furrowed in concentration. He looked up when he heard her approach, his expression softening ever so slightly. "Mother? What can I do for you?"

Evelyn closed the door quietly behind her, ensuring they wouldn't be overheard. She couldn't risk Celeste stumbling onto this conversation.

"We have much to discuss," Evelyn said, her voice low but firm. She moved to stand beside him, her hands clasping tightly in front of her. "It's about your sister."

Samuel leaned back in his chair, his eyes narrowing slightly. "Celeste? What's has she done now?"

Evelyn hesitated, choosing her words carefully. "She's not the same girl who left us, Samuel. Since she's come back, she's been different. She... she's trying to blackmail me."

Samuel's face darkened, his jaw tightening. "What are you talking about?"

Evelyn exhaled slowly, knowing she had to play this perfectly. "She's using something against me—an incident from years ago—to try and leverage her way into controlling the business. But that's not the worst part of it. She thinks she's untouchable, that she can manipulate all of us, starting with me." Her voice lowered, becoming more dangerous. "But we can't let her succeed in this. This family has faced many threats before, and we've always come out stronger. Celeste may think she's in control, but she has no idea who or what she's up against."

Samuel's eyes flickered with something unreadable, and then he spoke, his tone measured. "So, what do you need from me?"

"I need you to find someone. Someone off books your father can't know abut this. Someone who can follow her, watch her every move, and report back to us. Celeste is smart, but she's still young. She doesn't realize that we've been playing this game for far longer than she has."

Samuel nodded slowly, his gaze turning thoughtful. "She's underestimated you. And she's definitely underestimated me."

Evelyn felt a small sigh of relief. She had anticipated Samuel's loyalty, but it was always a gamble with him—his ambition often made him unpredictable. But in this moment, it seemed they were aligned. For now, at least.

"She wants to take control of the company, Samuel," Evelyn continued, her voice laced with urgency. "But if we act quickly, we can stop her before she gets too far. She can never be allowed to lead this family. It's not just about business. It's about everything we've built."

Samuel's eyes darkened with anticpation. "And she won't. I'll make sure of it."

Evelyn placed a hand on his shoulder, her grip firm. "Be careful. Celeste is playing a dangerous game, but she's still your sister. We need to be smart. We don't confront her directly. Not yet. We gather information, we find out what she's planning, and we move when the time is right."

Samuel's lips curved into a faint smile—one that didn't reach his eyes. "Don't worry, Mother. I'll handle it. I've already got the perfect person for the job."

Evelyn raised an eyebrow, intrigued. "And who might that be?"

"There's a man," Samuel said, leaning forward slightly. "Jack Dobson. He works for a security firm in the city. He's discrete, efficient, and he owes me a favor. I'll reach out to him tonight and have him start working on it. If she makes a move, we'll know about it."

Evelyn felt a sense of relief settle over her. Samuel was just as capable as she had hoped, and together, they would ensure that Celeste's ambitions never came into play. "Good. The sooner we get ahead of her, the better."

Samuel stood, straightening his jacket. "I'll take care of it, Mother. But what about Father? He's been blind to all of this."

Evelyn sighed, her expression softening for the first time since she had entered the room. "Your father... he's always had a blind spot when it comes to Celeste. He won't see what's happening until it's too late. But once we have the evidence, he'll have no choice but to face the truth."

Samuel nodded, his expression resolute. "We'll keep him in the dark for now. Until we have something solid."

Evelyn smiled faintly, the cold edge returning to her eyes. "Good. Just remember, Samuel—this is a family matter. We handle this quietly, and we handle it ruthlessly. Celeste may be clever, but she's still a child in this game. And we've been dealing with blackmail long before she even knew the meaning of the word."

Samuel smiled grimly. "She'll never see this coming."

As Samuel left the room to make the call, Evelyn stood in the silence, a new sense of control settling over her. Celeste may have thought she held the power now, but she had no idea what true power looked like.

Evelyn had spent her life traveling the treacherous waters of wealth and power, and no one—not even her own daughter—would strip her of what was rightfully hers. Celeste had made her first move, but Evelyn had learned long ago that the key to survival was patience. She would let her daughter believe she was winning, just long enough to set the perfect trap.

And when the time came, Celeste would discover that she was never going to be the head of this family.

# CHAPTER 8

The moon hung heavy over the Tomorrow mansion, casting a pale light through the windows that radiated throughout the mansion. Celeste stood in her room, her eyes fixed on her reflection in the mirror. Her lips were painted a soft crimson red, her hair perfectly put up—the very image of elegance. But behind the poised exterior lay a storm of emotions, carefully keeping them in check. She was no longer the daughter who sought approval or validation. She had tasted power, and she wanted more.

Her thoughts drifted to Victor Reynard.

Victor had always been a figure of shadow, someone her family had long buried in the past. Yet, he had returned for her, with promises that went beyond revenge. He offered her the chance to break free from her family's legacy, to take what was rightfully belonged to her. And now, she had her first weapon: the secret of Charlotte.

The phone rang softly, snapping her out of her racing mind. She picked it up with no hesitation.

"Celeste," came Victor's low voice on the other end, smooth and dripping with that dangerous charisma that had first drawn her in. "I take it you've confirmed the Charlotte secret?"

"Yes," Celeste replied, her voice even. "Mother all but admitted it. Charlotte is tucked away across the world with my father's child tucked in her arms, and my mother thinks she has done enough to conceal it."

Victor chuckled softly. "Good girl. Now, you know what has to happen next."

Celeste's jaw tightened. She had expected this, but it didn't make it any easier. "The file," she said, her voice devoid of emotion.

"Yes," Victor his voice strong. "The file. Your father has it locked away in his office. That file contains all the dirt on Charlotte's disappearance, and once we have it, your family will have no choice but to bend to our will. You'll control everything. Your father has been investigating it without your mother knowledge."

"There's just one problem," Celeste said, pacing the room. "My annoying brother has been glued to his side since I got back. He's suspicious. If I make a move, he'll know."

Victor's voice turned ice cold. "Then be smarter than him, Celeste. Distract him, manipulate him. Samuel may be ambitious, but he's no match for your wittiness. You've already proven that by getting this far. Don't get scared on me now."

Celeste inhaled deeply, composing herself. "I know. I won't. I have just the thing to get his attention. The file will be ours."

"Good," Victor said, his tone softening. "Remember, Celeste, we're in this together. If you want power, you'll need to fight for it. And no one—especially not your brother or your mother—can stand in your way."

The line went dead, and Celeste placed the phone back on the receiver. The wheels were turning quicker now, and with every conversation, every piece of leverage she gained, she felt her control becoming more soild. But she wasn't foolish. She knew Samuel and her mother were not far behind her. Evelyn, especially, had grown more wary with each passing day. But Celeste had her father exactly where she wanted him—wrapped around her finger.

Her thoughts were interrupted by a knock on the door. "Celeste, are you awake?" came her father's voice.

She quickly crossed the room, adopting the sweet, innocent expression she had perfected since she was a child. Opening the door, she smiled softly. "Of course, Father. Come in."

Carter Tomorrow stepped inside, a man who still radiated power and confidence even in his age. But there was something else in his eyes when he looked at her—adoration, a blind love that Celeste had come to rely on.

He sat on the edge of her bed, a thoughtful expression on his face. "I spoke to your mother today. She had some concerns."

Celeste's stomach twisted. She already knew where this conversation was headed. "About what?"

"She thinks you're... up to something," Carter said, his brow furrowing. "Evelyn's been on edge lately, more than usual.

She says you've been different, secretive. She even hinted that you might be trying to undermine me." He paused, looking directly into her eyes. "Now I have to ask is any of this true?"

Celeste held back a smirk, allowing only a flicker of shock and hurt to cross her face. "Father, I'm surprised. Mother's always been suspicious of me. But this?" She shook her head, letting her voice crack slightly for full effect. "I've done nothing but try to reconnect with everyone since I came back. Is it really so hard to believe that I've changed for the better?"

Carter's expression softened immediately, just as she knew it would. "I didn't mean to upset you, sweetie. It's just... you've been through so much. We all have. I don't want any more turmoil in this family."

She sighed, sitting down beside him. "I understand. Mother's always been protective of the family and the business, but maybe she's projecting her own fears onto me. I know she's been stressed, especially with the business." She hesitated, giving him a pointed look. "And Samuel... he's been so territorial. It's like he doesn't want me to have any part in the family business."

Carter frowned. "Samuel has been difficult, hasn't he?"

"He's just scared that I might actually be good at it," Celeste said softly, her eyes wide and sincere. "I want to help, Father. I want to prove that I can be a part of this family's legacy. But Samuel... he's so persistent."

Carter rubbed his chin, nodding thoughtfully. "I'll talk to him. Don't worry, sweetheart. You'll have your place in the family, just like you deserve. After all you are my little girl"

Celeste smiled, the perfect mask of gratitude hiding the victory she felt swelling up inside her. "Thank you, Father. That means so much to me."

As he stood and kissed her forehead, Celeste watched him leave the room. She had played him perfectly, as she always did. He was so blinded by his love for her that he couldn't see the obvious truth, that she had become something far more dangerous than the sweet girl he thought he knew.

But Evelyn knew. And Samuel was on to it too.

The real game was heating up now. She would have to act quick, to get that file from her father's office before Samuel caught on. He was watching her every move, and she had to stay a step ahead. Victor was right—if she wanted to control this family, she had to outmaneuver them all.

Celeste stood by the window, looking out at the vast expanse of the estate. It was all within her reach, but the next few days would determine everything. She could feel the pressure mounting, the tension in every room of the house. Her family might think they could had her figured out, but they had never faced her like this before—cold, manipulative, and ready to take everything.

Her mother had tried to warn her father, but she had underestimated how well Celeste could play the role of the loving daughter. And Samuel? He was smart, but too attached to the old ways, too confident that he could manage the situation. He had no idea that Celeste had already begun setting traps for him.

The game was on, and no one would be safe from the fire she was about to unleash.

# CHAPTER 9

The darkness of the Tomorrow mansion extended long into the night, the silence thick and almost suffocating. Samuel Tomorrow sat in his father's study, the fire crackling the only source of sound. It was late, but sleep had long abandoned him. Since his mother's warning about Celeste, a seed of doubt had taken root deep inside him, gnawing at his inner thoughts.

Carter had always been firm but fair. Samuel was the eldest, the one who should inherit everything, yet his father's favoritism toward Celeste had become obvious. She had never been interested in being involved in the family business until after the kidnapping. Their father, who was blind to her schemes and manipulation, fell deep under her spell due to Celeste's sudden drastic change in behavior.

He shifted uncomfortably in the large leather chair, thinking about his last conversation with his father. The one where Carter had almost taken Celeste's side. Samuel had tried to convince him that something was amiss, that Celeste was up to something tainted, but Carter had brushed him off, saying Samuel was being paranoid. It was Evelyn's doing, his father had said. Evelyn had planted these ideas in his head.

Samuel felt the weight of those words. A rift was forming, and it was getting deeper with every passing day. His father, the man he had always looked up to, the man who had taught him everything, was now slipping away. And it was all because of Celeste.

The fire flickered, casting long shadows across the room, and Samuel stood, restless. He needed answers, needed proof of what Celeste had her hands into. He needed to find a way to expose her before she could gain any more control than she already had.

As he paced the room, something caught his eye—the sound of soft footsteps approaching. His heart quickened. The hour was late, and no one should be awake. Narrowing his eyes, Samuel moved toward the door, cracking it open just enough to peer into the dimly lit hallway.

There, moving silently toward their father's office, was Celeste.

She was dressed in a black silk robe, her hair pulled back, her movements intentional and cautious. Samuel's pulse raced. What was she doing? He watched as she glanced over her shoulder, then disappeared into their father's private office.

A deep sense of dread settled over him, but it was quickly replaced by bitterness and anger. He knew it—knew she was up to something. Without hesitation, Samuel slipped into the hallway and followed, moving as quietly as he could. He waited just outside the door, listening for any sign of what she was doing.

Inside, Celeste moved with precision. She knew exactly where her father kept the key to his safe, hidden behind the large portrait on the wall. With a quick, practiced motion, she lifted the painting and retrieved the key. The lock clicked softly, and she opened the safe, her heart racing as she reached for the folder.

This was it. The file on Charlotte. The file that would solidify her control over the family, and with Victor's help, bring down the empire that had once belonged to her father.

But before she could savor the victory, a voice broke the silence.

"What do you think you're doing, Celeste?"

She froze her hand still inside the safe. Slowly, she turned to see Samuel standing in the doorway, his eyes blazing with fury.

For a moment, neither of them spoke, the tension between them thick as the air.

"I could ask you the same thing," Celeste said, her voice cool, her fingers tightening around the folder.

Samuel stepped forward, his fists clenched. "I knew you were up to something, but this? You've gone too far."

Celeste didn't flinch, didn't betray a single ounce of fear. "I'm doing what needs to be done. You wouldn't understand."

Samuel's eyes narrowed. "Understand what? That you're trying to steal from Father? That you're trying to undermine everything this family has built?"

Celeste's lips curled into a small, knowing smile. "Steal? No, Samuel. I'm taking what's mine. And if you think you can stop me, then you're more delusional than I thought."

Samuel crossed the room in a few quick strides, grabbing her arm before she could leave. "You're not going anywhere with that file."

Celeste's eyes flashed with something dark and dangerous as she yanked her arm free. "Let go of me. You don't even know what is in here, do you?"

For a moment, they stood inches apart, the weight of their sibling rivalry threatening to explode. Samuel had always been the poster child, the heir apparent, but now Celeste was challenging that, threatening his place in the family. And it enraged him.

"I do, and it's none of our business. You think you can just take my rightful place as the heir?" Samuel growled. "You think Father will just let you waltz in here and poison everything?"

Celeste's smile widened. "Oh, Samuel. You still don't get it, do you? Father hardly even pays you any mind anymore. He only sees and cares for me. You think you'll be the heir once Father finds out he has another son?"

Samuel's grip tightened. "You've poisoned him against all of us." You won't win sister. I am going to make it my mission to take you down. I am going to stand by and let you destroy this family.

"You don't have a choice, my dear brother. I will be victorious. It's best you just let me be. It will be easier for all of you."

"Forget it. I am not going to stand with you. You will fall. And I will be there to celebrate your demise."

"Your choice," she said cackling.

As she walked away. Samuel watches her fade into the darkness of the mansion. His blood was boiling by this point and he couldn't help but feel like she may just be right. He felt that his mother would cave into her demands and the war between them would only be bloody.

# CHAPTER 10

The heavy hum of the city echoed around Celeste as she stood in a dim alleyway, hidden by the shadows. The night was cool, but her palms were sweaty, and her heart raced as she clutched the file tighter under her arm. She had been waiting for this moment for what felt like an eternity. Every step she had taken since coming home, every careful manipulation, had led to this exchange.

From the end of the alley, a figure emerged from the darkness—Victor Reynard. His sharp, cold eyes glinted in the dim streetlight, and his expression was unreadable as he approached.

"Did you bring it?" Victor's voice was smooth, almost casual, as if they were discussing nothing more than a business deal.

Celeste handed the file over without a word. Her heart was pounding, but she kept her face neutral. She had risked everything to get this, and now she had to fully commit to Victor's plan. As he took the file from her hands, a sense of worry pricked at the back of her mind. She hated relying on someone else—hated trusting Victor—but this was the only way to secure her place at the head of the family operations.

Victor flipped through the file with a slight smirk playing on his lips. "I have to say, Celeste, I didn't think you'd pull it off. Your father's office... That's no small feat."

"Samuel caught me," Celeste said, her voice tight. "But he doesn't know the extent of what's in the file. He knows I'm up to something, but he has no idea just how far this goes."

Victor raised an eyebrow, looking up from the documents. "Samuel is a problem. If he's onto you, we need to make sure he stays out of the way. At least for now."

Celeste crossed her arms. "That's why I'm here. Already taken care of. But, I know him. He won't let it go. He is having me followed. I managed to avoid detection getting here."

Victor closed the file, his smirk turning into something darker, more dangerous. "Consider it done. I'll have my people make sure Samuel is... preoccupied for a while. He won't interfere with our plans."

Celeste nodded, relieved. "Good. He's been a thorn in my side since I got back. I can't move forward with him watching my every step."

Victor stepped closer, his eyes never leaving hers. "You've done well, Celeste. But remember, this is just the beginning. We still need to be mindful. One wrong move, and the whole plan could collapse."

She swallowed, feeling the weight of his words hang over her. "I know. But I'm not going to lose. Not to Samuel, not to my mother, and certainly not to my father. This is my time, Victor."

Victor chuckled softly. "That's the spirit."

As they exchanged a brief, tense glance, Celeste turned on her heel, ready to leave the alley and return to the mansion. But the feeling of being watched gnawed at her again. She had felt it earlier in the day—like eyes on the back of her neck—but had brushed it off as paranoia. Now, she wasn't so sure if she managed to avoid being followed.

Unbeknownst to her, a man lurked in the shadows not far from where she and Victor stood. He had been watching the whole exchange, just as Samuel had instructed. Samuel had been smart enough to suspect Celeste wasn't working alone, and now, thanks to this hired spy, Samuel had the confirmation he needed.

Victor Reynard was alive.

As Celeste disappeared down the street, the man snapped a few photos with his camera, catching clear shots of Victor's face. He smirked to himself, as he prepared to drive away. He had what Samuel needed.

Back at the mansion, Samuel sat in his study, circling. His conversation with Celeste in their father's office played on loop in his head, taunting him. The way she had looked at him, the way she had twisted everything... She was spiteful and cunning. He had known that from the moment she came back, but now, he had proof.

The door to his study creaked open, and the man he had hired slipped inside. He didn't speak as he dropped the photographs on the desk in front of Samuel.

"Victor Reynard," the man said, his voice low. "Your sister is working with him."

Samuel's eyes narrowed as he picked up the photos, each one a perfect shot of Victor and Celeste standing together in that alley. His heart pounded in his chest as he stared at the proof. The file was irrelevant now. The fact that Victor was alive and working with Celeste changed everything.

"So, it was all a setup," Samuel muttered, more to himself than to the man. "The kidnapping, her return... It was all a scheme to manipulate us, to manipulate Father."

The man nodded. "Looks that way. Your sister's been playing a dangerous game. Victor's not exactly known for being forgiving."

Samuel's mind raced. If Victor was involved, that meant the stakes were deadlier than he had imagined. The kidnapping had been nothing more than a ruse, a way for Celeste to worm her way back into the family and into their father's favor. And now, she was using Victor to take down the rest of them. His father, blinded by love for his daughter, couldn't see what was happening right under his nose.

Samuel gritted his teeth. "Celeste thinks she's got it all figured. She thinks she can manipulate us all and get away with it. But she's in for a surprise. I won't let her destroy this family."

The man raised an eyebrow. "What's the plan?"

Samuel leaned back in his chair, his mind already working out the next steps. "We let her think she's in control for a little while longer. But now that I know Victor's alive, we have leverage. And when the time is right, we'll expose them both."

The man nodded, his face grim. "You sure you can handle it? Your sister... She's dangerous."

Samuel's eyes hardened. "She's dangerous, yes. But she's also reckless. She's made a mistake by working with Victor. And when she falls, it'll be from a height so great, she'll never recover."

The man nodded, slipping back out of the room without another word, leaving Samuel alone with his thoughts. He stared at the photos again, the rage inside him bubbling to the surface. His father had always told him that the family's legacy was everything, and Samuel had dedicated his life to upholding that legacy. Celeste had thrown it all away for her own selfish ambitions, and he couldn't allow that.

She thought she could silence him, manipulate him the way she had manipulated their father. But she had no idea just how deep the game was going. He now knew Victor was alive, and with that knowledge, he had a weapon far more dangerous than any secret Celeste held over him.

His sister had underestimated him, and soon, she would realize just how much of a mistake that was.

# CHAPTER 11

The morning sun streamed through the heavy curtains of the Tomorrow mansion, casting long, golden beams into Samuel's bedroom. He lay awake, staring at the ceiling, his mind tangled in the chaos of the night before. The knowledge that Victor Reynard was alive weighed on him like a stone in his chest. His sister, the same girl who used to follow him around the mansion as a child, was now plotting the family's downfall alongside one of the most dangerous men they had ever crossed.

He knew he had to act. But for the moment, all he could think about was Maria.

Maria—her name brought a flood of memories to his mind, memories he wasn't proud of. The secret affair, the hidden glances, the late-night rendezvous that had started so innocently, but had quickly turned into something much darker. He had allowed himself to become vulnerable with her, allowed his feelings to cloud his judgment. He had trusted her.

But trust had no place in this world, not when it came to the Tomorrows.

He swung his legs over the edge of the bed and stood, running a hand through his hair. Maria hadn't shown up for work that morning. No one had seen her in the house for the last few days. Samuel had assumed she had taken a few days off or had been dismissed by the staff for some small mistake. But now, in the cold light of day, something gnawed at him.

Celeste.

Had his sister made good on her promise? She had threatened him in their father's office and made it clear that she knew about his secret. But even Celeste wouldn't have gone so far as to... remove Maria, would she?

A sick feeling settled in the pit of his stomach as he threw on his clothes, his mind racing. He needed to know where Maria was, needed to make sure she was safe.

Victor Reynard's hideout was a far cry from the luxury of the Tomorrow estate. Hidden deep within the city's underbelly, it was a place where deals were made in shadowed rooms and alliances were broken with a single bullet. And it was here, in this dark world, that Maria had returned.

She stood by Victor's side, the man who had once controlled her every move, her every thought. She had tried to escape this life, had tried to find something real with Samuel. But real didn't exist when you were a pawn in the hands of people like Celeste and Victor.

Victor leaned against the table, the file Celeste had given him spread open before him. He glanced at Maria with an amused smile, his cold eyes never leaving her face.

"You did well," he said, his voice as smooth as silk. "I almost thought you'd gone soft with that little romance of yours."

Maria didn't respond, keeping her fixed on the floor. She had been so foolish to think she could escape this life, so naïve to believe that Samuel could protect her. From the beginning, she had been placed there by Celeste's careful design, recommended as house staff by Celeste herself. Samuel had no idea that every whisper he'd shared with her, every intimate moment, had been fed back to Celeste.

Victor pushed away from the table and moved closer to her, his breath warm against her ear. "You understand your place now, don't you?"

Maria nodded, her heart pounding in her chest. She had tried to love Samuel, but love had no place in a world like this. She had chosen her path, and now she was back where she belonged—under Victor's control.

Victor's smile widened. "Good. Because now, we have work to do. Celeste is depending on us, and you've proven your loyalty. But I need more from you, Maria. I need you to make sure Samuel stays out of the way permanently."

Maria stiffened, her breath catching in her throat. "What do you mean?"

Victor's eyes darkened. "Samuel's becoming a problem. Celeste wants him out of the picture. And you, my dear, are the key to making that happen."

A chill ran down Maria's spine. She had known this day would come, but part of her had hoped it wouldn't. She had played her role, had fed Celeste the information she needed, but this.. this was different. Samuel may have been a fool, but he didn't deserve to die for it.

"I... I can't," she stammered, her voice barely a whisper.

Victor's expression hardened, his hand gripping her chin and forcing her to look at him. "You don't have a choice, Maria. You never did. Either you finish what you started, or you'll end up like the rest of the people who cross me."

Maria's heart pounded as she looked into Victor's cold, dead eyes. She knew he meant every word, knew that there was no escape from him. She had tried to build a life with Samuel, but that life was nothing more than an illusion.

"I'll do it," she whispered, the words tasting like ash on her tongue.

Victor released her, a satisfied smile playing on his lips. "Good girl. Now, go. Celeste is expecting you to finish this."

Back at the mansion, Samuel searched for any trace of Maria. He asked the staff and checked her quarters, but it was as if she had vanished into thin air. Every inquiry was met with the same response: She no longer works here.

Frustrated and anxious, Samuel stormed through the hallways, his mind spinning. Something was wrong—deeply wrong. And every instinct told him that Celeste was behind it. He headed toward his father's office, determined to confront Celeste once and for all.

But as he neared the door, he overheard voices. Quiet, hushed, but unmistakable.

"... She did her job well," Celeste was saying, her voice calm, calculating. "Samuel is distracted, and Maria has returned to Victor. He'll take care of her from here."

Samuel froze, his blood running cold. His worst suspicions were confirmed—Maria had been working for Celeste all along. The affair, the confidences, everything had been a lie. She had been a spy, feeding information to his sister while pretending to care for him. And now, she was back with Victor, the man he had thought dead.

The revelation hit him like a punch to the gut, but it was quickly replaced by a seething rage. Celeste had played him. She had used Maria to manipulate him, to keep him distracted while she enacted her plans. And now, she was going to have Maria killed—or worse.

Without thinking, Samuel burst into the office, his face twisted with fury. Celeste, sitting behind their father's desk, didn't even flinch at his sudden entrance. Instead, she looked up with a small, knowing smile.

"Samuel," she said, her voice laced with mock concern. "Is everything all right?"

His hands shook as he pointed a finger at her, his voice trembling with rage. "You... you set me up. You used Maria to spy on me. You've been feeding Victor information this whole time!"

Celeste's smile widened, her eyes glinting with satisfaction. "Oh, Samuel. You always were so predictable. I didn't need Maria to spy on you. You've been so blinded by your ambition, by your desire to be Father's heir, that you missed the real game happening right under your nose."

Samuel's chest heaved with anger, but Celeste remained calm, almost bored by his outburst.

"What's the matter, brother?" she asked, leaning back in the chair. "Can't handle a little betrayal?"

Samuel's fists clenched at his sides. He had underestimated Celeste and had thought he could outmaneuver her, but now, it was clear. She would stop at nothing to claim her place at the head of the family—even if it meant destroying everyone in her path.

And Maria... Maria was just another casualty in her ruthless ascent.

But this wasn't over. Not yet.

"I'll stop you," Samuel hissed, his voice low and dangerous. "You think you've won, but you don't know me, Celeste. I'll bring this whole plan crashing down around you."

Celeste's smile faded, her eyes narrowing. "You can try, Samuel. But you're already too late."

With that, she turned back to the file on the desk, dismissing him as if he were nothing more than an inconvenience.

# CHAPTER 12

The tension in the Tomorrow mansion had reached a boiling point, but no one on the outside could sense it. The grand dinners, the elegant parties, and the polished smiles continued as if nothing was amiss. Yet beneath the surface, a battle was being waged between Celeste and Samuel—each trying to outmaneuver the other while keeping their father, Carter Tomorrow, blissfully unaware.

In the halls of the mansion, Samuel's rage simmered beneath a composed exterior. He knew that confronting Celeste head-on would only tip his hand, and his father was far too enamored with his daughter to see her for what she was. Samuel had to play the game carefully, pretending to play the dutiful son, while quietly plotting his next move. Celeste, meanwhile, wore her mask of sweetness even more convincingly. She laughed at the dinner table, charmed the staff, and played the perfect daughter for Carter. But behind closed doors, her mind was spinning with strategies.

She had always known that her alliance with Victor Reynard was a temporary one. He was dangerous, yes, but he was also predictable in his ambition. He needed her now, but that wouldn't last. When he no longer found her useful, he wouldn't hesitate to cast her aside or worse—eliminate her. That's why Celeste had begun to dig deeper, investigating the things Victor didn't know about. This was more than just a simple play for control of the family. There was something bigger here, something about her father's empire that went beyond blackmail and business deals.

And then she found it.

It had started as whispers in the business papers and through contacts in Washington—something about the new deal her father had struck in Venezuela. The South American country had been the focus of attention for oil giants for years, but only recently had Carter secured an exclusive contract for labor and extraction rights. At first glance, it appeared to be a golden opportunity, a massive source of revenue for the Tomorrow family.

But as Celeste started to peel back the layers, she realized the truth was far darker.

The labor practices her father had been enforcing in Venezuela were not only ruthless but illegal. Washington had started to catch wind of it—rumors of bribes, corruption, and even the use of forced labor. Workers in Venezuela were reportedly being treated as little more than slaves, forced into grueling hours under harsh conditions with little pay. And those who tried to speak out? They were silenced, sometimes permanently.

The more Celeste uncovered, the more she realized that her father wasn't just complicit—he was the architect of this entire operation. He had built his fortune on the backs of the exploited, using his wealth and influence to keep the law at bay. But Washington's suspicion had been growing, and it wouldn't be long before someone decided to make a move. If this scandal broke, it wouldn't just ruin Carter—it would ruin the entire Tomorrow empire, leaving it vulnerable to vultures like Victor.

Celeste stared at the stack of papers she had assembled in her private study, her mind racing. This could be her key, the leverage she needed to take control. With this information, she could bring her father to his knees without needing Victor's help. But it also meant treading very carefully. If her father or Samuel caught wind of what she was doing, it could all fall apart.

She closed the file and locked it in the drawer, leaning back in her chair. She knew she had to keep this information hidden from Victor, at least for now. He might be her ally, but she wasn't stupid enough to trust him with everything. When the time came, Victor would have to be dealt with, too. He had made her life a game of survival, and for that, he would pay.

Celeste smirked at the thought. She hadn't forgotten the way he had kidnapped her, extorted her, and forced her into this dangerous game. He thought he held all the cards, but in truth, he was just another pawn on the board. And when the time was right, she would make sure he knew it.

Meanwhile, Samuel was feeling the weight of his growing disconnect from their father. Despite Carter's attempts to reassure him that everything was under control, Samuel could feel his grip on the family business slipping. Celeste had wormed her way back into their father's good graces, charming him with her flattery and apparent loyalty. But Samuel wasn't fooled. He knew his sister well enough to know she was up to something—something dangerous.

After overhearing the conversation about Maria, Samuel had begun his quiet investigation. He had put out feelers, contacted old business partners, and even gone to trusted family lawyers, trying to uncover any trace of what Celeste was planning. But so far, she had been careful, keeping her secrets hidden behind a carefully constructed facade.

Frustrated, Samuel poured himself a glass of whiskey in his father's office, staring out the large windows overlooking the sprawling estate. The place had always felt like a fortress to him, a symbol of power and security. But now, it felt like a prison.

His father's voice rang in his head, words from their last conversation. *"Don't worry about Celeste. She's doing what's best for the family. You should learn to trust your sister."*

Trust. That word meant nothing anymore, not in this house. Celeste was hiding something, and Samuel was determined to find out what. But every step he took seemed to lead him further into the dark, and now, he wasn't sure if he could trust anyone—not even his father.

His thoughts were interrupted by the sound of footsteps behind him. Samuel turned to see his sister standing in the doorway, her face a picture of calm. But Samuel knew better. Behind those cool eyes, there was a storm brewing.

"Samuel," she said, her voice smooth and practiced. "I was hoping to talk to you."

Samuel raised an eyebrow, setting his glass down on the desk. "About what? How you've been plotting behind my back?"

Celeste's smile didn't falter. "Don't be so dramatic. I think we both know that we're on the same side here. We're both trying to protect the family, even if we don't always agree on how."

Samuel's jaw clenched, but he said nothing, letting her continue.

"I've been doing some digging into Father's latest ventures," she said, her tone casual. "Particularly the deal in Venezuela."

Samuel's interest piqued, but he kept his expression neutral. "What about it?"

"There's more going on than what Father's telling us," Celeste said, stepping closer. "Washington is watching him closely. If they find out the extent of what's happening down there, it could destroy us. Father's keeping secrets, Samuel. And those secrets are going to cost us everything if we're not careful."

Samuel narrowed his eyes. "Why are you telling me this?"

Celeste's smile grew sharper. "Because I think we both know that Father's time is coming to an end. The future of this family lies with us. But if we're going to take control, we need to be united."

Samuel studied her, trying to read between the lines. He didn't trust her, but there was no denying that she was onto something. The Vansuela deal had always seemed too good to be true, and if Washington was involved, things would be worse than he had imagined.

But there was something else, something she wasn't saying. And Samuel wasn't about to be manipulated again.

"I'll think about it," he said finally, his voice cold.

Celeste's smile never wavered. "Good. Just remember, Samuel—we're stronger together. And if you're not with me, you're against me."

With that, she turned and walked out of the office, leaving Samuel alone with his thoughts. The war between them was far from over, and both of them knew it. But for now, they had to keep playing their parts, pretending to be the perfect children while secretly plotting each other's downfall.

The game was still in motion, but the stakes were higher than ever. And in the end, only one of them could win.

# CHAPTER 13

Evelyn Tomorrow sat in her study, sipping tea while a storm of unease brewed within her. The stately mansion was quiet, too quiet for her liking. She had sensed it for weeks now—something shifting between her children. Samuel had grown cold, keeping secrets from her, and Celeste... Celeste was becoming a stranger before her very eyes. It was clear they were hiding something, and whatever it was, it threatened the very foundation of their family.

Evelyn's instincts had always been sharp, honed from years of safeguarding her family's reputation. But now, she felt an unfamiliar panic rising. She was no longer in control. Samuel had hired someone to follow Celeste, claiming it was for her protection, but Evelyn knew better. He was keeping her out of conversations, withholding information. And then there was Celeste—drifting further away, her once sweet demeanor replaced by cold calculation.

What they didn't know was that Evelyn had started her investigation. If her children were scheming, she needed to be two steps ahead. And so, she quietly reached out to her contacts, piecing together what they refused to tell her. She uncovered whispers, dark rumors about Victor Reynard, and the devastating truth that he was alive—and pulled the strings behind Celeste's kidnapping.

But the discovery that chilled her to her core was that Victor now knew the secret Evelyn had spent decades burying: Charlotte.

Evelyn's hands trembled as the memory surfaced. Charlotte, the child Carter had fathered during an affair, the daughter Evelyn had been sent away to Europe before Carter could ever learn of her existence. Evelyn had covered it up, a shameful secret buried beneath layers of deception. But now, that secret had surfaced. Victor had found her. And Charlotte wasn't just living quietly abroad—she had a son.

Evelyn stood from her chair, her chest tightening. She couldn't let this ruin everything. The years of carefully crafted lies were unraveling, and if Charlotte's existence came to light, it wouldn't just destroy her—it would tear the entire family apart.

Her only option was to confront Victor, to strike a deal before he could use Charlotte as a weapon against her. But time was running out. Victor had been waiting for this moment, and Evelyn knew she had to move quickly before everything she had worked so hard to protect came crashing down.

The meeting was arranged in a run-down warehouse on the outskirts of Chicago. Evelyn had come alone, just as Victor requested. She couldn't risk involving anyone else—not Samuel, not even Carter. This was her secret to bear.

As she entered the dimly lit space, Victor was waiting for her, leaning against a steel table with a predatory grin.

"Evelyn Tomorrow," he greeted her, his voice dripping with satisfaction. "I knew you'd come."

She kept her face neutral, though her heart was racing. "You know why I'm here, Victor."

"Oh, I know *exactly* why you're here," he said, pushing off the table and circling her like a wolf stalking its prey. "You've kept your husband in the dark for years, haven't you? About his precious little daughter, Charlotte."

Evelyn's pulse quickened, but she remained steady. "What do you want, Victor?"

Victor smirked. "You already know what I want. Carter's empire, everything he's built—it's all about to crumble, thanks to you. You thought you could hide Charlotte forever? Send her away before Carter found out she was pregnant? And now she has a son. Your grandson, Evelyn."

Evelyn's heart dropped at the mention of Charlotte's son. She had never met him, but she had done everything to keep them hidden, to shield Carter from the truth. The stakes had never been higher.

"Let's make a deal," she said, her voice calm but laced with desperation. "You let Celeste go, and I'll give you what you want. Information, names, anything. Just... leave my family out of this."

Victor chuckled darkly. "Your family? Oh, Evelyn, you've already lost them. Celeste has been lying to me, but that's not your real problem, is it?"

Evelyn's breath hitched. "What are you talking about?"

"Charlotte," he said, leaning in closer. "She's not dead. She's very much alive, tucked away in Europe, raising your husband's child. And now, she's *my* leverage."

The world seemed to tilt beneath Evelyn's feet. Victor had her right where he wanted her, and there was no escape.

"You're not leaving here, Evelyn," Victor continued, his voice menacing. "Not until I get what I want. You thought you could keep this secret from Carter forever, but now, I'm going to use it to destroy him. And you're going to help me."

Evelyn's throat tightened, her mind racing. She had walked into Victor's trap, and now, she was a pawn in his game. But worse than that, Charlotte's existence, and her son, were no longer just shadows of her past—they were weapons in Victor's hands.

Before she could speak, Victor's tone shifted. "You're staying here, Evelyn. You won't be leaving. And I don't need Celeste anymore. She's been lying to me, playing her own game, and I'm done with her."

Her heart sank. Victor had figured out Celeste's deception. And now, with Evelyn as his hostage, he didn't need Celeste to finish his plan.

The game had shifted, and the Tomorrow family was on the verge of collapse. As Victor's men closed in, Evelyn realized the true extent of the danger she was in. There was no one left to help her—not Carter, not Samuel, not even Celeste.

And Victor was about to destroy them all.

# Chapter 14

Charlotte White stepped off the train, the scent of the city filling her lungs with a strange nostalgia. It had been years since she left Chicago, years since Evelyn Tomorrow banished her to Europe to keep Carter's affair hidden. But now, she was back. Her sharp eyes flickered over the crowd as she made her way through the bustling station, her heart steady and determined. No longer the young, naive assistant, Charlotte had returned with a plan—and she wasn't alone.

Victor Reynard had promised her the opportunity for revenge, and she took it. They shared the same enemy: the Tomorrow family. It was time to dismantle their empire, piece by piece, starting with the man who had betrayed her.

Charlotte's thoughts sharpened as she recalled her reunion with Victor. The day she returned to the city, he had found her waiting at the edge of the Tomorrow estate, watching. His presence, dark and calculated, had given her a sense of purpose.

"The time is coming, Charlotte," Victor had said. "Carter won't see it coming. And neither will the others."

She smiled at the memory, thinking of how easy it had been for them to concoct their scheme, playing on the weaknesses of each family member. Now, it was only a matter of time before they all fell.

Celeste's heels clicked against the marble floor of Victor Reynard's penthouse as she let herself inside. She was furious. Victor had cut her off, severing the thread of their dangerous partnership without so much as an explanation. She wasn't used to losing control, not after the way things had been going since her return to the family. With each secret she uncovered about her father's dealings, with each lie that unraveled before her, she felt more powerful. Victor had been the key to her plans, the catalyst for her betrayal.

But now he was gone. And she needed him.

As she stepped into the dimly lit living room, Victor emerged from the shadows, dressed in a crisp, tailored suit, his gaze unreadable.

"You've been avoiding me," Celeste said, her voice cold, but her pulse quickened as his eyes locked on hers.

"I had to make sure you could handle things on your own," Victor replied, his tone smooth, detached. "You're not the same girl I brought back. You're stronger now, more dangerous."

Celeste's anger softened, but she didn't lower her guard. "You didn't need to test me."

"You needed to prove yourself," he said, stepping closer, his eyes studying her. "And you did."

The tension in the air shifted, becoming something darker, and more intimate. Celeste felt the pull between them, the unspoken connection that had always simmered just below the surface. She had fought it for weeks, refusing to let her feelings cloud her judgment, but now, standing before him, everything seemed to fall away.

She reached out, grabbing his collar, pulling him close, the frustration of the past weeks boiling over. "Don't ever cut me off again," she whispered.

Victor's eyes darkened, and in a swift movement, he pulled her against him, their lips colliding in a kiss that burned with the fire of all their unspoken desires and resentments. Celeste's mind raced, but her body acted on its own, surrendering to the moment. It was reckless, dangerous—everything she had sworn to avoid. But it also felt inevitable.

As they parted, breathless, Victor's hands still gripping her arms, he whispered, "You and I, Celeste, we're going to destroy them. Together."

Celeste smiled, her anger dissolving as a new plan formed in her mind. "Then let's start with my brother."

Across town, Charlotte was busy setting her plan in motion. The years had hardened her, and now, she was more than just a scorned lover. She had power. As she entered the hotel suite where Victor had arranged to meet, she found him sitting by the window, his fingers tracing the edge of a glass of whiskey.

"You're late," Victor said, without turning to face her.

"I had a few things to take care of," Charlotte replied, her voice cool as she sat across from him. "Besides, we're in no rush. Carter doesn't even know I'm back yet."

Victor smirked. "He won't be the first to fall, you know. Celeste is already playing the game, and Samuel... well, we both know he's too ambitious for his good."

Charlotte leaned back in her chair, studying him. "And Celeste? Can you control her? She's becoming more dangerous than either of us thought."

Victor's gaze flicked toward her, his eyes narrowing. "I don't need to control her. She's right where I want her."

Charlotte raised an eyebrow, sensing something different in Victor's tone. There was something more than just business in the way he talked about Celeste. A spark of jealousy flickered within her, but she quickly buried it. This wasn't about Victor or even Celeste. This was about taking down the Tomorrow empire, one piece at a time.

"Good," Charlotte said, her voice steady. "Because when the time comes, I want to be there to see Carter fall."

Victor raised his glass. "You will, Charlotte. And when it's over, the Tomorrow family will be nothing but a memory."

As their glasses clinked, sealing their pact, the darkness that surrounded them seemed to close in tighter. The game was in motion, and the pieces were beginning to fall into place.

Neither Charlotte nor Celeste would stop until they had taken everything—and everyone—down.

# CHAPTER 15

Celeste stood before the tall mirror, adjusting the collar of her blouse. The reflection in the mirror wasn't her own anymore—it was a woman shaped by secrets, by quiet deals whispered in the dark. Her hands trembled slightly as she fixed her hair, though not out of fear. She had no choice now but to see this through.

A knock came at the door, soft, almost tentative.

"Come in," she called, turning around as Victor Reynard stepped inside, his face a mixture of calm and intensity.

He closed the door behind him. "Are you ready for tonight?" His voice was low, laced with the tension that had been simmering between them since their arrangement began.

Celeste nodded, her pulse quickening as Victor's gaze lingered on her. She had been playing this dangerous game, but every time she looked at him, the lines blurred. She told herself it was all for power—control over her father's empire—but there was more to it. There was something about

Victor, something magnetic, that made her want to be near him.

Victor stepped closer, his fingers brushing against her cheek. "You've done well so far, Celeste. Your father's blind to what's happening right under his nose. Soon, the real game begins."

Celeste smirked. "I told you, I'll get what I want. But don't mistake this for anything more than business."

Victor leaned in, his breath warm against her skin. "And yet," he whispered, "you haven't pulled away."

She didn't. Instead, Celeste tilted her chin up, meeting his lips in a heated kiss. This was dangerous. She knew it. But it was also thrilling. The line between desire and ambition blurred as Victor's hands slid around her waist, pulling her closer. For a brief moment, the weight of her family's secrets and the dark plot she'd spun melted away. There was only Victor, the heat between them, and the sense of power it gave her.

But as quickly as it started, Celeste broke the kiss, pulling back with a sharp breath.

"We can't," she muttered. "Not now."

Victor raised an eyebrow. "Are you sure? Because it seems like you want this more than you're willing to admit."

"I want my father's empire," she replied coldly, her heart pounding, but her voice steady. "This... is just a distraction."

Victor studied her face, then slowly backed away, his eyes still lingering on her. "As you wish. But don't forget, distractions can be very useful in our line of work."

Celeste said nothing, watching him leave the room. Once the door clicked shut, she leaned against the wall, trying to regain her composure. She couldn't let herself get too close to him. Not now, when everything was on the line.

Downstairs, Samuel paced the mansion's hallway, his brows furrowed. Something had been nagging at him all day—his mother's absence. Evelyn had been acting distant lately, almost as though she were hiding something. And then there was Celeste. She had returned from her kidnapping with a new, icy demeanor that he couldn't shake. It was as though she had come back a stranger.

He had asked around, but no one seemed to know where his mother was. That alone unsettled him.

"Where is she?" Samuel muttered under his breath.

His father, Carter, sat in his study, flipping through papers when Samuel entered.

"Father, have you seen Mother?" Samuel asked, his voice tense. "I haven't seen her all day."

Carter waved a hand dismissively. "Oh, don't worry about her, Samuel. She went shopping with Celeste earlier. They'll be back before nightfall."

Shopping with Celeste? Samuel frowned. That didn't sit right with him. His mother hated going anywhere with Celeste these days. Something felt off.

"I don't know, Father," Samuel insisted. "Mother's been acting strange. Ever since Celeste came back, something's changed. Have you noticed it?"

Carter sighed, barely looking up from his papers. "You're overthinking things, son. Your mother is fine. Celeste is fine. You're worrying about nothing."

Samuel's frustration grew. How could his father not see what was right in front of him? There was something deeper happening, something he needed to figure out before it was too late.

"I hope you're right," Samuel said, though doubt lingered in his voice.

Later that evening, Samuel wandered through the mansion, unable to shake the uneasy feeling in his chest. His footsteps echoed softly against the marble floors as he passed by the grand foyer. And that's when he saw her—Maria, the housemaid, standing at the edge of the room as though she had just appeared out of thin air.

"Maria?" Samuel called, stepping toward her. "Where have you been? You've been gone for days."

Maria's eyes darted nervously around the room before she answered, her voice low. "I had... some matters to attend to."

Samuel narrowed his eyes. "What matters? Why are you avoiding me?"

"I'm not avoiding you, Mr. Samuel," Maria said, her voice shaking slightly. "It's just that... things have been complicated lately."

Samuel's suspicion deepened. Something wasn't right with Maria either. She had always been loyal to the family, always reliable. But now she looked... different. Nervous.

"Complicated how?" he pressed. "What's going on, Maria?"

Maria hesitated, glancing over her shoulder before speaking again. "Things are happening in this house, Mr. Samuel. Things you don't know about."

Samuel felt a chill run down his spine. "What things? What do you know?"

But before Maria could answer, a loud knock came from the front door, cutting through the tense air like a knife. Maria flinched, her face pale.

"I have to go," she whispered, hurrying off before Samuel could stop her.

Samuel watched her disappear down the hall, his mind spinning. The unease gnawed at him, more vicious than ever. There were too many secrets being kept, and too many people hiding things. And he was determined to uncover them all—no matter what it took.

# CHapter 16

C arter Tomorrow's eyes flicked to the clock on his office wall, his heart beating in a frantic rhythm that had nothing to do with the heat of the late Chicago summer. Evelyn had been missing for over 24 hours, and no one—not the staff, not their children, not even his closest associates—knew where she was.

Washington was circling him like a vulture, and now this. His empire was crumbling, piece by piece.

His phone buzzed with another call—one of his lawyers, no doubt—but he ignored it. Instead, he rose from his desk, raking a hand through his salt-and-pepper hair as he paced the room. The office felt too small, too suffocating as if the walls were closing in on him.

How had it come to this? Evelyn, his constant anchor, was always so precise, so careful. She wouldn't just disappear. And yet, no one had seen or heard from her since yesterday morning. She hadn't even called. Carter had hoped, initially, that she was simply taking one of her unannounced retreats—Evelyn often vanished to their beach house or some quiet estate to clear her head when things at home became too tense.

But this... this was different. She had never been gone this long without a word.

He strode out of the office and down the hall toward the drawing room, where Samuel and Celeste had been holed up. The staff had been tight-lipped all morning, offering only confused looks and murmured denials. None of them had seen Evelyn since she left for her morning walk in the garden. That had been her routine for years—always so predictable, so dependable.

But now? Now she had vanished.

As Carter approached, he could hear Celeste's soft, measured voice from within the room. She was speaking with Samuel, likely discussing some mundane family matter. They had no idea what was coming.

He flung the door open with a force that surprised even him. Celeste and Samuel looked up, startled by his sudden entrance.

"Has anyone seen your mother?" Carter demanded, his voice taut with barely suppressed panic.

Samuel frowned, standing from his chair. "No, Father. We haven't seen her since yesterday. The staff said she didn't come back after her walk."

Carter turned to Celeste, his eyes narrowing. "And you? Have you spoken to her?"

Celeste raised an eyebrow, leaning back in her chair with an almost casual demeanor. "I haven't seen her since last night. Is something wrong?"

Carter could barely contain his frustration. His daughter was so calm, so unaffected. It unnerved him, but there was no time to think about that now. "She's been gone for more than a day. This isn't like her."

"Maybe she's just taking a break," Celeste said, her voice cool and detached. "You know how she gets."

Samuel shot Celeste a warning look. "This is serious, Celeste."

Carter's mind raced, barely registering their exchange. He turned and stormed toward the main foyer, where several of the household staff lingered, trying to appear busy. He cornered one of the senior housekeepers, his voice low but fierce.

"Mrs. Halloway, I want you to gather every member of the staff. I need to know if anyone saw anything unusual yesterday. Any detail, no matter how small. And if any of you are lying to me—"

"Of course, Mr. Tomorrow," Mrs. Halloway interrupted quickly, her hands trembling slightly. "But I assure you, we've all been looking. No one saw her after she left the garden."

Carter ran a hand down his face, trying to suppress the rising tide of anxiety threatening to break his composure. Where the hell was Evelyn? He turned and headed toward his office again, hoping to find a lead—anything—waiting on his desk.

But as he sat down, his mind wandered back to something else that had been gnawing at him for weeks. The federal agents investigating him. Washington was watching, closing in on his deals, his money, and his carefully constructed empire. And now his wife had gone missing at the worst possible moment.

He had kept the investigation quiet, away from his family. Not even Samuel knew. He couldn't risk it. His empire—built over decades of manipulation, influence, and secrets—was being threatened from all sides, and his family was oblivious. If word got out, if his enemies discovered how close the government was to unraveling his financial schemes, they would tear him apart.

For now, he had managed to stall the investigation with his lawyers, but it was only a matter of time before the walls closed in. And now, with Evelyn missing, it felt like everything was collapsing at once.

A knock at his door interrupted his spiraling thoughts. It was Samuel.

"Father, you need to take a step back," Samuel said as he entered, his expression calm but firm. "We'll find her. She's probably just... taking some time away."

Carter's eyes flashed. "Do you think she'd just disappear for no reason? Evelyn doesn't leave without telling anyone. This isn't one of her trips."

Samuel hesitated for a moment, his brow furrowed. "No, but panicking isn't going to help."

Carter stood, his frustration boiling over. "You don't understand. There's more going on than you know, Samuel.

If Evelyn doesn't come back soon... if we don't find her... everything I've built could fall apart."

Samuel's expression shifted, his eyes narrowing slightly. "What do you mean? What aren't you telling me?"

Carter paused, realizing he had said too much. But how could he explain the gravity of the situation without tipping his hand?

"Just... trust me," Carter said, his voice lower now, almost pleading. "Things are happening that you don't need to worry about. But I need to find your mother before it's too late."

Samuel studied his father for a long moment, suspicion growing in his eyes. "Is this about the business?"

Carter waved him off, his frustration mounting again. "Don't worry about it, Samuel. Just focus on finding Evelyn. I've already questioned the staff. You need to start making calls—anyone she might have spoken to. We need answers."

Samuel hesitated but nodded, sensing that his father was holding something back. He left the room without another word.

Carter sank into his chair again, rubbing his temples as the weight of everything pressed down on him. Washington. Evelyn. His family. It was all crashing down around him, and he was running out of time to fix it.

His phone buzzed again, but this time, the name on the screen made his blood run cold.

It was Victor Reynard.

Without hesitating, Carter answered, his voice steady but edged with fury. "Where is she?"

Victor's laugh came through the line, low and mocking. "You're slipping, Carter. I thought you'd have figured it out by now."

Carter's grip tightened on the phone. "If you've touched her—"

"Relax," Victor interrupted smoothly. "Your wife is fine... for now. But if you want her back, you're going to have to play this game by my rules."

Carter's pulse pounded in his ears. "What do you want?"

There was a pause, and then Victor's voice turned icy. "I want you to lose everything, Carter. And I'll start with your wife."

The line went dead.

Carter dropped the phone, his heart hammering in his chest. His worst fears had been confirmed.

Evelyn was in Victor Reynard's hands.

And now, so was he.

# CHapTer 17

Celeste stood in the dimly lit warehouse, the smell of dust and damp concrete heavy in the air. In the far corner, Evelyn was tied to a chair, her head slumped forward. The once-mighty matriarch of the Tomorrow family looked small, vulnerable—a shadow of the woman who had controlled so much for so long. But despite the ropes that bound her, Celeste knew the real danger wasn't her mother's physical presence—it was her mind. Evelyn's brilliance, her manipulation, and her mastery of secrets had ruled their family for decades.

And now, it was Celeste's turn to break that rule, but on her own terms.

Charlotte, pacing nearby with the confidence of someone who thought she had the upper hand, was completely unaware of the trap being set for her. Celeste watched her carefully, every step calculated, every movement precise. Charlotte had believed she was orchestrating Evelyn's downfall—foolish, really. There was no room for outsiders in this family feud. Charlotte didn't understand what it meant to be a Tomorrow.

But Celeste understood.

Victor stood at Celeste's side, his eyes gleaming in the half-light. He had always planned to release Evelyn, but that part of the scheme had remained between him and Celeste. Charlotte was nothing more than a pawn, thinking she was playing the queen's game when she was merely a sacrificial piece.

"Are you sure about this?" Victor's voice was low, teasing, as he leaned toward Celeste. His fingers grazed her waist lightly, sending a ripple of heat through her. There was something intoxicating about their partnership—his dangerous charm, her ice-cold ambition. Together, they were unstoppable.

"Of course," Celeste replied smoothly, her eyes never leaving Charlotte. "My mother's destruction is my privilege. No one else gets to do that—not Charlotte, not you."

Victor smirked, his lips brushing against her ear. "That's what I love about you, Celeste. Always playing the long game."

Celeste's lips curled into a smile. She turned to face him, catching his dark gaze. "I don't just play the game, Victor. I *win* it."

Their lips met, a brief, heated exchange that left her heart racing, the adrenaline of the moment mixing with the thrill of their shared power. She pulled away, her mind snapping back into focus. There would be time for more later—when they had everything they wanted.

Charlotte, oblivious to the tension between the two of them, turned from Evelyn and strode toward them. "Everything's ready," she said, her tone dripping with anticipation. "It's time to break her."

Celeste watched her with thinly veiled contempt. Charlotte was so sure of herself, so confident in her ability to bring Evelyn to her knees. But she didn't understand. This wasn't her fight.

"I'll handle it from here," Celeste said, her voice cool but firm. "You've done enough."

Charlotte frowned, suspicion flickering across her face. "We're not done yet, Celeste. Your mother hasn't given us what we need."

Celeste's eyes hardened. "She will. But you won't be the one to get it from her."

"What are you talking about?" Charlotte demanded, her voice rising. "I've risked everything for this! I'm the reason she's here in the first place."

Celeste took a step forward, her gaze unwavering. "And now you're done. This is my family, my legacy. You're an outsider, Charlotte. You were never going to finish this. That's my job."

For a moment, Charlotte was silent, her face twisting in disbelief. Then her eyes darkened with fury. "You're double-crossing me?" she hissed. "After everything I've done?"

Celeste's smile was cold and sharp. "You were always just bait. You just didn't realize it."

Charlotte's eyes flashed with rage, but before she could react, Victor moved swiftly, grabbing her arm and pulling her back. "Careful, Charlotte," he said, his voice laced with mock sympathy. "You wouldn't want to make things worse for yourself."

Charlotte struggled against his grip, her eyes blazing. "You think you can just push me aside? I'll tear your whole family apart!"

Celeste took another step forward, her voice dropping to a deadly whisper. "No, you won't. You've done your part, Charlotte. Now it's time for you to go."

Victor's grip tightened on Charlotte, and with a swift motion, he shoved her toward the exit. Charlotte stumbled but caught herself, her face twisted with fury and disbelief. "You'll regret this, Celeste," she spat. "I'll make sure of it."

"Good luck," Celeste said, her voice cold and detached as Charlotte stormed out of the warehouse, the heavy door slamming behind her.

For a moment, there was silence. Then Celeste turned back to her mother, who had lifted her head slightly, her eyes focused and calculating despite the situation. Evelyn's lips curled into a small, knowing smile.

"I see you haven't lost your touch," Evelyn said, her voice low but steady.

Celeste crossed the room, her heels echoing against the concrete floor. She stopped in front of her mother, looking down at her with a mixture of anger and admiration. "You always taught me to take control," Celeste said softly. "To play the game better than anyone else."

Evelyn's smile widened, though there was a flicker of something darker in her eyes. "You've certainly learned that lesson well."

Victor moved to stand beside Celeste, his presence solid and commanding. His hand brushed against Celeste's again, a silent affirmation of their shared victory.

"We're letting you go, Mother," Celeste continued, her voice steady. "But this isn't over. You're not free. You'll never be free—not until I say so."

Evelyn's gaze flickered between Celeste and Victor, understanding dawning in her eyes. "You've aligned yourself with him," she said, her tone almost amused. "A dangerous move."

Celeste's lips curled into a smirk. "No more dangerous than you aligning yourself with Father."

Evelyn let out a soft chuckle, shaking her head. "I suppose that's true."

Victor stepped forward, his voice calm and authoritative. "Your time here is up, Evelyn. We'll release you, and you'll go back to your life. But things will be different now. You'll answer to Celeste, not the other way around."

Evelyn's eyes narrowed, but she remained silent. She knew better than to fight back—at least not now.

Victor and Celeste turned to leave, the weight of their shared power hanging in the air between them. As they stepped out into the cool night, their hands brushed once more, and Celeste looked up at him, her pulse quickening.

Their partnership had shifted, from a mere alliance of convenience to something deeper, something more dangerous. The lines between ambition and desire were blurring, and

Celeste couldn't deny the pull she felt toward him—toward the power they wielded together.

Victor glanced down at her, his dark eyes gleaming with the same fire that burned in her chest. "We've only just begun," he said softly, his voice laced with promise.

Celeste smiled, her heart racing. "I know."

# CHAPTER 18

Evelyn Tomorrow limped through the grand doors of the Tomorrow mansion, her body battered and bruised, but her pride unbroken. The staff rushed toward her, their eyes wide with shock and concern, but she waved them off with a terse flick of her wrist.She wasn't ready to be coddled. She wasn't ready for questions. And, above all, she wasn't ready to admit what had truly happened.

Evelyn had made her choice to protect Celeste. She couldn't expose her daughter, not yet, even though she knew Celeste had orchestrated the entire ordeal. The betrayal burned deep inside her, but the sting of it was dulled by something else-a strange, bitter pride. Celeste had learned from the best, after all.

Samuel stood at the base of the grand staircase, watching his mother closely. His sharp eyes didn't miss the way she held herself-her movements slow and deliberate, as if masking the pain. He knew something was off. Something far deeper than what anyone could see.

"Mother," Samuel said cautiously, stepping toward her. "Are you alright?"

Evelyn met his gaze, her expression composed but shadowed. "I'm fine, Samuel.It's nothing I can't handle."

He raised an eyebrow, suspicion flickering across his features. He could feel it-feel that his sister had something to do with this.Celeste's absence, her strange calmness in the past few days, it all pointed to something darker lurking beneath the surface.

"Where's Celeste?" he asked quietly, his voice laced with accusation.

Evelyn's eyes flickered for a moment, but she quickly recovered. "She's handling business.Your sister is always looking out for this family."

Samuel didn't say anything. He couldn't, not without proof. He knew his father would never believe him. Carter was already consumed with rage, his mind set on finding Victor Reynard and taking him down for good. The idea that Celeste was involved was something Samuel knew Carter couldn't handle.

As if on cue, Carter stormed into the hallway, his face twisted with fury. His eyes landed on Evelyn, and for a moment, his anger softened, replaced by concern for his wife."Evelyn," he breathed, rushing to her side."I'll kill him for this. I'll make Victor pay for what he's done to you."

Evelyn winced, but not from the physical pain. She couldn't tell him that Victor was not the real threat-not anymore. That would unravel everything. "It's too risky, Carter," she said softly, her voice a mixture of weariness and warning. "He's dangerous. You need to be careful."

But Carter shook his head, his fists clenching at his sides. "I'm not afraid of that coward.He attacked me once already. I won't let him get away with it again."

Samuel watched the exchange, the tension rising between them. He didn't trust the silence surrounding Celeste's involvement, but he knew better than to challenge it outright-not yet. His father wouldn't believe it, and his mother was protecting something larger. For now, Samuel had to bide his time.

"Victor isn't your only problem, Father," Samuel said quietly, catching Carter's attention. "We don't know what's really going on here."

Carter turned toward Samuel, his eyes narrowing. "What are you suggesting?"

Samuel hesitated, knowing that planting any seeds of doubt about Celeste would be dangerous, especially without proof. "Just that we should be careful. Victor isn't the only one with a motive."

Before anyone could respond, a loud knock echoed through the mansion, interrupting the rising tension. The sound reverberated through the hall, sharp and insistent.

Carter frowned and motioned to one of the housekeepers to answer the door, but before they could reach it, Samuel stepped forward."I'll get it," he said, a sense of foreboding washing over him.

As he pulled open the heavy oak door, his heart skipped a beat.

Charlotte stood on the doorstep, her face twisted with a mix of determination and fury.She looked disheveled, like someone who had been plotting revenge in the shadows for far too long. The sight of her alone sent a cold shiver down Samuel's spine.

"Charlotte?" he breathed, unable to mask the shock in his voice.

But it was Carter who reacted first, his face hardening as his eyes darkened with recognition. "What the hell are you doing here?"

Without waiting for an answer, Evelyn pushed past Carter, her face contorted in rage as she advanced toward Charlotte. Her wounds, both physical and emotional, were forgotten in the heat of the moment.

"You!" Evelyn snarled, her voice dripping with venom. "How dare you show your face here after everything!"

Charlotte didn't flinch. Instead, she stepped inside with a confidence that bordered on arrogance. "You think you're the only one who's suffered, Evelyn? You and your family have been playing games with everyone's lives for years. Now it's time for the tables to turn."

Before anyone could react, Evelyn lunged at Charlotte, her hands flying toward her in a violent, desperate attack. Years of hidden resentment, pain, and betrayal exploded in that moment. The two women collided in a flurry of fists and fury, their screams echoing through the mansion as they fought like wild animals.

"Evelyn, stop!" Carter yelled, grabbing for his wife's arm, but she was too far gone, too enraged to be controlled.

Charlotte fought back just as fiercely, clawing at Evelyn's face, her words sharp and cutting. "You think you can take me down? You think you can protect your perfect little family from the truth?"

Evelyn snarled as she threw Charlotte against the wall, the sound of the impact ringing in the air. "I'll kill you before you destroy my family!"

Samuel and Carter stood frozen for a moment, shocked by the raw violence between the two women. But it was Carter who finally acted, pulling Evelyn away from Charlotte and holding her back.

"Enough!" Carter barked, his voice thundering through the room. "This is not how we handle things!"

But Evelyn, still seething, broke free from Carter's grip. Her eyes locked on Charlotte, who was now slumped against the wall, panting and glaring back at her. "You'll never take us down, Charlotte. Never."

Charlotte wiped blood from the corner of her mouth and laughed darkly. "We'll see about that."

As the tension thickened, Samuel caught the glint in Charlotte's eyes. She wasn't finished—not by a long shot. This was just the beginning, and whatever she had planned, it was going to rip through their family like a storm.

But there was another truth hidden beneath the surface, one that only Samuel suspected.

His sister was at the center of all of it, pulling the strings. And soon, he would have to face that reality head-on, even if it meant confronting Celeste herself.

# CHAPER 19

Carter stood by the grand window of his study, sipping his whiskey as he watched the sunset over the Tomorrow estate. The golden hues lit up the Chicago skyline in the distance, but his mind was elsewhere. The visit from his Washington ally had been short, but the implications were significant.

"Smooth sailing," the man had said, his voice dripping with hidden meaning. "The oil process in Venezuela... it's been going more smoothly than expected. You've done well, Carter."

The words echoed in Carter's head. On the surface, it was praise. But there was a subtle reminder that it was all built on a delicate foundation. The Washington ally left him with a firm handshake and a knowing look, the weight of their political and financial dance lingering in the air.

As Carter swirled his drink, his eyes darkened. He wondered if everything was truly as smooth as it seemed—or if someone was pulling strings behind his back.

Down the hall, Celeste and Evelyn's voices clashed in the drawing room, rising above the usual quiet of the mansion. Samuel had been passing by when he heard it—Celeste's sharp tone, followed by his mother's more measured response. Curious, he moved closer, careful to stay out of sight.

"I don't know how you think you can control all of this," Celeste hissed. "You're as blind as Father is. He doesn't even know what's really happening."

"I know far more than you think, Celeste," Evelyn shot back, her voice cool but firm. "And you're walking into dangerous territory. I don't need to remind you how quickly things can fall apart when people play with fire."

"Victor knows about the meeting, Mother. What do you think he's going to do with that information?"

Evelyn went silent for a moment, her composure barely wavering. "You think I care about your little arrangement with him? You think you're in control? You've always underestimated what I know. Don't be so naive."

Celeste scoffed. "You're in over your head, and when this all collapses, you'll be the one to blame."

Samuel's heart raced. He had suspected that his sister and mother were hiding something, but hearing it spelled out like this? It was the perfect opportunity.

Stepping into the room, Samuel cleared his throat. Both women turned toward him, their expressions unreadable.

"Mother, Celeste," he greeted coolly. "Interesting conversation."

Evelyn's eyes narrowed, but she remained calm. "Samuel, this is a private matter. You shouldn't be listening."

"I wasn't listening," Samuel lied smoothly. "I just happened to overhear something that piqued my interest." He turned his gaze to his mother, his voice hardening. "It seems like you've been keeping a lot from us. And now it's time to choose—me or Celeste."

Evelyn's expression remained neutral, but her eyes flashed with anger. "I have nothing to choose between. You have no idea what's coming our way, Samuel. You think you can play games, but you don't understand the stakes."

"Oh, I think I do," Samuel replied coldly. "Celeste isn't trustworthy. She's been working with Victor. She's playing all of us, and if you're not going to do anything about it, then I will."

Evelyn stepped forward, her voice low but steady. "You're walking into dangerous waters. Don't think you can handle what's coming just because you think you've found a way to back me into a corner."

Samuel studied his mother's face, searching for cracks in her calm exterior, but Evelyn was as unreadable as ever. His eyes flicked to Celeste, who was watching the exchange with a guarded expression. He knew she wouldn't go down without a fight.

"Just remember," Evelyn continued, her voice like ice, "this family is built on secrets. And if you push too hard, you might be the one to bring it all down."

Later that night, Carter sat in his study, reviewing the details from the Washington meeting. But his mind kept wandering back to his family. There had been whispers in the house for weeks, subtle shifts in the way Evelyn and Celeste interacted. Samuel had been more tense than usual too, asking questions he wouldn't normally care about. Something was off.

As he stared at the papers in front of him, Carter couldn't shake the feeling that he was being kept in the dark. He glanced up as Samuel entered the room, a determined look on his face.

"Father, we need to talk," Samuel said, sitting down across from him.

Carter sighed, leaning back in his chair. "What is it this time, son?"

"It's Celeste," Samuel began, his voice low but insistent. "She's hiding something. I overheard her talking with Mother earlier. They're covering something up, and I think it has to do with Victor Reynard."

Carter's brow furrowed. "Victor?"

"Yes," Samuel pressed. "Celeste is playing both sides, and I'm not sure where Mother stands in all of this. But they're keeping something from us—something big. You can't ignore it anymore."

Carter frowned, his mind racing. He had always trusted Evelyn, even when she kept her distance, and Celeste... well, he had his suspicions about her since her return. But Samuel had never been one to sound the alarm unless he was sure of something.

"You really believe this?" Carter asked, his voice tinged with doubt.

Samuel nodded. "I know it. And if you don't start asking the right questions, this family is going to implode."

Carter sat in silence for a long moment, the weight of Samuel's words sinking in. He had always been the one in control, the one who knew everything. But now, for the first time, he wasn't so sure. Maybe Samuel was right. Maybe there was more going on than he had been willing to see.

Finally, Carter spoke, his voice grim. "I'll look into it. But if you're wrong, Samuel..."

"I'm not wrong," Samuel cut in firmly. "Just... don't let her fool you."

As Samuel left the room, Carter sat in the growing darkness, the shadows creeping in as his thoughts churned. Something was happening beneath the surface, something that could tear his family apart if he didn't act quickly. And for the first time, he felt a cold suspicion settle in—maybe Celeste wasn't the daughter he thought she was.

# Chapter 20

Charlotte stood before the mirror, smoothing her dress as she prepared for what would be the most dangerous move of her life. She had stayed silent for too long—years of hiding in the shadows, living with the secret that Carter Tomorrow, the man who had built his empire on power and control, had a son he didn't know existed.

Her heart raced as she recalled the way Evelyn had sent her away to Europe, covering up the affair, hiding the pregnancy, and ensuring that Carter remained ignorant. But no more. The time had come to reveal the truth, and this time, Celeste wouldn't stand in her way.

With one final breath, Charlotte left her room and headed toward Carter's study. She had waited for years for this moment, and now she would no longer be silenced.

Carter was going through paperwork when Charlotte entered, unannounced. He barely looked up, too engrossed in the details of his business deals. But Charlotte's presence commanded attention.

"Charlotte?" His eyes narrowed, confusion clouding his face. "What are you doing here?"

She stood tall, a quiet strength radiating from her. "We need to talk, Carter. There's something you need to know—something I should have told you a long time ago."

Carter sat back in his chair, his brows furrowing. "What are you talking about?"

Charlotte's voice was steady, though her heart raced. "We have a son, Carter. You and I. I was pregnant when I left for Europe. Evelyn knew, and she's been keeping it from you all these years."

The room went silent, the weight of her words crashing down on him. Carter's face drained of color as the realization set in.

"A... son?" he repeated, his voice barely a whisper. He leaned forward, his hands gripping the arms of the chair. "You're telling me... I have a son?"

Charlotte nodded. "Yes. And it's time you know the truth. He's out there, and he deserves to know who his father is."

Carter stood, pacing the room, his mind spinning. This was a betrayal he hadn't expected—not from Evelyn, not from Charlotte. His life had been meticulously controlled, every detail accounted for, but this? This was a revelation that shook him to his core.

"Why now?" he demanded, his voice rising. "Why tell me this now?"

Charlotte's eyes hardened. "Because Celeste is playing a dangerous game, Carter. She's in league with Victor Reynard. If you don't stop them, everything you've built will fall apart.

I've kept quiet long enough, but I won't let Celeste destroy you. Not anymore."

Carter's mind raced. Charlotte's revelation was like a puzzle piece falling into place, and suddenly, everything seemed clearer. Celeste had always been ambitious, but this? To align herself with Reynard? He had underestimated his daughter.

He turned to Charlotte, his voice cold. "Does anyone else know?"

Charlotte shook her head. "Not yet. But they'll figure it out soon enough. You need to act before it's too late."

Meanwhile, Celeste and Victor had grown uneasy. The tension between them was palpable as they sat in one of Victor's private offices downtown, the city lights glowing beneath them.

"Carter's getting suspicious," Victor muttered, lighting a cigarette. "He knows something's off. I saw the way he looked at me during that last meeting."

Celeste crossed her arms, her face set in a scowl. "He doesn't know anything—yet. But we need to be careful. Samuel's been snooping around, too. I caught him watching me the other day. He's onto us."

Victor blew out a stream of smoke, his eyes narrowing. "Samuel's always been too curious for his own good. He's not a threat. But if Carter starts digging, we'll have a problem."

Celeste felt a chill run down her spine. She knew the stakes were high, but with Victor, she had always believed they could outmaneuver her father. Now, though, with Samuel getting closer, everything felt more precarious.

"We need to make our move soon," Celeste whispered. "Before they figure out what we're planning."

Victor nodded, but his eyes were far away, already calculating their next step.

Samuel had followed Celeste through the streets of Chicago, careful to stay far enough behind that she wouldn't notice. He had grown increasingly suspicious over the past few days, piecing together her strange behavior with the conversations he'd overheard. Tonight, he had seen her slip out of the mansion, heading straight into the heart of the city, and he knew something was up.

When she entered a nondescript building, Samuel waited a few moments before quietly following her inside. The halls were dark and quiet, the soft hum of conversation barely audible behind closed doors. As he made his way closer, he heard Celeste's voice, low and conspiratorial. Then, another voice—Victor's.

He peeked around the corner just in time to see them together—Victor's hand on Celeste's waist, their lips meeting in a passionate kiss.

Samuel's heart sank. It was worse than he had imagined. His sister wasn't just conspiring with Victor; she was in a full-blown relationship with him.

Before Samuel could move, he felt a heavy hand on his shoulder. He spun around to see one of Victor's men standing behind him, a smirk on his face.

"Well, well," the man said. "Looks like someone's been snooping."

Samuel's stomach lurched. Before he could react, the man grabbed him, dragging him down the hall and into the room where Victor and Celeste stood. Both of them turned in surprise as Samuel was thrown to the floor.

"Samuel," Celeste said, her voice cold and calm. "What are you doing here?"

Victor loomed over him, a predatory grin spreading across his face. "Looks like the boy couldn't mind his own business."

Samuel glared up at them, his chest heaving with anger and fear. "I knew something was wrong with you," he spat, looking directly at Celeste. "Mother warned me, but I didn't listen. Now I understand—this was all part of your plan, wasn't it? You knew I'd eventually follow you."

Celeste knelt down beside him, her expression unreadable. "You've always been too curious, Samuel. And now you're in over your head."

Victor crossed his arms, watching the scene with amusement. "What should we do with him?"

Celeste stood, her gaze never leaving Samuel's. "We keep him here—for now. We have bigger problems to deal with."

As they left the room, Samuel lay there, the weight of realization crashing down on him. His family was falling apart, and he was at the center of the storm.

# CHAPTER 21

The heavy silence in the Tomorrow mansion was palpable as Carter stormed into the sitting room where Evelyn sat, calmly reading. Her posture was poised, but the moment she looked up and saw the fury in his eyes, her expression faltered.

"We need to talk," Carter growled, barely containing his rage. "Now."

Evelyn set her book down slowly, her fingers trembling just slightly. "Carter, what's going on?"

"Charlotte," he spat, pacing back and forth like a caged animal. "You sent her away when she was pregnant with my child. You hid my son from me!"

Evelyn's eyes widened momentarily before narrowing, her calm mask slipping into one of calculated defense. "I did what I had to do, Carter. She was a distraction, a threat to everything we've built. You don't know what it was like—"

"I know enough!" Carter interrupted, his voice trembling with fury. "You had no right. No right to keep that from me."

Evelyn rose from her chair, her voice rising to match his. "I had every right! You think this family runs on love and loyalty? It runs on power, on secrets! And I wasn't about to let some affair ruin everything we've worked for!"

Their shouting echoed through the mansion, and neither of them noticed Charlotte emerging from Carter's study. She stood at the doorway, silent, until Evelyn's gaze fell on her.

"You," Evelyn hissed, her face twisting with anger. "What are you doing here? Haven't you caused enough damage?"

Charlotte stepped forward, her chin held high. "I've come to take back what's mine. You kept me hidden, you sent me away like I was nothing, but that's over now. I'm not leaving again, and this time, Carter knows everything."

Evelyn's composure shattered. "You think you can just waltz back in here and take control?" Her voice was shrill, and her hands shook with barely contained rage. "This is my family. My legacy. You're nothing more than a footnote in our history."

But Charlotte didn't flinch. For once, Evelyn wasn't the one holding the cards.

"I've already won," Charlotte said coolly, her voice steady. "You can fight all you want, but the truth is out. Carter knows about our son. And soon, so will everyone else."

Evelyn's eyes blazed, but before she could respond, Carter stepped between them, his voice dark and final. "It's over, Evelyn. You've controlled this family long enough. I'm done."

For the first time, Evelyn looked as though she had lost control—her world crumbling right in front of her. She could see Carter slipping away, and with him, the power she had so carefully curated over the years.

But she wasn't done yet.

Without another word, Evelyn stormed out of the room, her heels clicking sharply against the floor. She had to get away, to think. As she passed through the halls, something gnawed at her—a sense that something else was wrong.

Samuel. She hadn't seen him all day.

Meanwhile, at Victor Reynard's private estate, Samuel sat tied to a chair in a dark room. His face was bruised, his breathing labored. Celeste stood nearby, watching with a cold detachment as Victor circled her brother like a predator toying with its prey.

"You always thought you were the smart one, didn't you, Samuel?" Victor sneered, lighting a cigarette and blowing the smoke into the air. "Always thinking you could outplay the game."

Samuel glared up at him, his lips cracked and dry. "You won't get away with this. Father will come for me."

Celeste smirked, stepping closer. "Father won't know where to find you. And even if he did, he's got bigger problems now."

Victor leaned in, his face inches from Samuel's. "You see, Samuel, this has been in the works for a long time. You were just too blind to see it."

Samuel's heart sank as the pieces finally came together. His mother's warnings, Celeste's coldness, Victor's sudden reappearance—it had all been orchestrated. He had walked right into their trap.

Back at the mansion, Evelyn frantically searched for Samuel. Her anger had given way to dread as she realized he was nowhere to be found. She cornered a servant, demanding to know if they had seen him.

"Not since this morning, ma'am," the servant stammered, fear in her eyes.

Evelyn's chest tightened. Something was terribly wrong. She rushed back to the sitting room, where she found Charlotte and Carter together again, speaking in low tones.

Without even acknowledging Charlotte, Evelyn grabbed her coat and keys. She had an idea where Samuel might be. And if she was right, she had only one move left to play.

The drive to Victor's estate felt longer than it should have. Evelyn's mind raced with possibilities. She couldn't lose Samuel—he was the key to holding the family together. As she pulled up to the large iron gates, a sense of dread washed over her. This was it. Everything was about to come to a head.

Inside, Victor and Celeste were waiting when Evelyn stormed in, her eyes flashing with fury.

"I want to see my son," she demanded.

Victor smiled, a cruel smile that didn't reach his eyes. "Your son? Well, Evelyn, that's a bit complicated, isn't it?"

Evelyn's gaze shifted to Celeste, who stood by Victor's side, arms crossed. "This has gone too far," she said, her voice low but dangerous. "Let Samuel go, or I'll make sure both of you regret it."

But Celeste's expression remained cold, detached. "You're not in control here, Mother."

Victor stepped forward, his voice smooth and taunting. "You came here to make a deal, didn't you? What do you have to offer, Evelyn?"

For the first time in years, Evelyn felt truly powerless. She had always been the one pulling the strings, manipulating events from behind the scenes. But now, she was at the mercy of her own daughter and the man she had tried to keep out of her life for so long.

But Evelyn was nothing if not resilient. She straightened her shoulders and met Victor's gaze with steely resolve. "If you still want to make a deal, then let's talk."

Celeste's eyes narrowed as she watched her mother. She had never seen Evelyn like this—desperate, yes, but also calculating. There was still something dangerous in her, something that made Celeste hesitate.

Victor smiled, sensing the tension. "Then let's see what you're willing to sacrifice."

# CHapTer 22

The dim light flickered above Samuel, casting long shadows on the concrete floor of Victor Reynard's underground chamber. His body ached from the beatings, his mind racing through a dozen different scenarios—none of them ending well for him. Yet, through the pain and confusion, one thing had become clear: Celeste was his only way out.

Celeste stood across from him, her arms crossed, watching him like a hawk. Victor leaned against the wall, a smug grin on his face, but for the moment, it was Celeste who held the cards.

"You're smarter than I gave you credit for," Celeste said, her voice cold but thoughtful. "You didn't run to Father with your suspicions. You came to me."

Samuel clenched his fists, pain rippling through his sore muscles. "I didn't come here by choice. I'm your prisoner."

Celeste raised an eyebrow. "Prisoner? No. You're still family, Samuel. But you were bound to get in the way."

Samuel's jaw tightened. "So, what now? You keep me locked up until you and Victor destroy everything Father built?"

Celeste shook her head slowly, a small, calculating smile creeping onto her lips. "No. I'm willing to make a deal."

Samuel blinked, caught off guard. "What kind of deal?"

Celeste took a step closer, her voice dropping to a near-whisper. "You walk away from all of this. The family business, the power struggle, everything. In return, I make sure you stay alive—and you won't have to explain to Father why you were sniffing around my personal affairs."

Samuel narrowed his eyes. "And why would I do that? What's in it for me, besides living another day?"

Celeste tilted her head, giving him a long, unreadable look. "Because I know something you don't."

Samuel's heart skipped a beat. He had learned to read Celeste over the years—she was always ten steps ahead, always holding something back. "What are you talking about?"

A sly smile curled her lips. "Mother isn't as innocent as you think. She didn't just send Charlotte away because she was some threat to the family's reputation. She sent her away because she was pregnant—with Father's child."

The room seemed to spin as the truth hit Samuel like a freight train. His father's affair with Charlotte, the secrecy surrounding her disappearance—it all made sense now. His entire life had been shaped by this one colossal lie.

"Father..." Samuel murmured, his voice trailing off as he struggled to process it all. "He had a child with Charlotte?"

Celeste's smile widened. "Yes. A son. And Mother covered it up, just like she's covered up so many things. You're not as blind to the family's inner workings as you think, but you still don't know everything."

Samuel's mind whirled, his anger at Celeste and Victor momentarily eclipsed by the sheer weight of the revelation. His family was more fractured, more broken than he had ever imagined. "And you've known this?"

Celeste nodded. "Of course. I've known for years. But it wasn't useful to me—until now."

Samuel clenched his fists, shaking his head. "So this is how you plan to control everything? Blackmail Father with his own secrets?"

Celeste shrugged. "It's not blackmail if it's the truth, Samuel. Father has been living a lie, and now it's all coming to light. The question is—what are you going to do with that truth?"

Samuel paused, the tension between them thick in the air. Celeste had laid out her terms, and now it was his move. He could walk away, let his sister and Victor take control, or he could stay and fight. But with this new knowledge, he realized the stakes were much higher than he'd thought.

"I'll make a deal with you," Samuel said, his voice steady. "But I want something in return."

Celeste raised an eyebrow, intrigued. "And what would that be?"

"I'll keep my mouth shut about everything," Samuel said. "But you make sure Mother doesn't go down with you. She's not innocent, but she doesn't deserve whatever you're planning."

Celeste considered his request for a moment before nodding. "Done. But you better hold up your end of the bargain."

Back at the Tomorrow mansion, the tension between Carter and Charlotte had finally begun to settle into something resembling conversation. Carter paced the study, trying to make sense of everything that had been revealed. The existence of his son—the secret Evelyn had kept for so many years—had shaken him to the core.

Charlotte stood near the fireplace, watching him carefully. She knew Carter well enough to know that he was still reeling, still processing the bombshell that had just dropped on his carefully curated life.

"Why didn't you tell me sooner?" Carter asked, his voice low and strained.

Charlotte exhaled softly. "I wanted to, Carter. But Evelyn... she made sure I couldn't. You know how she is—how she controls everything."

Carter stopped pacing, turning to face her. "And now? Why are you telling me now?"

Charlotte hesitated for a moment before deciding to reveal the final piece of her truth. "Because there's something else you need to know, Carter. Something about Celeste."

Carter's brow furrowed, confusion flashing across his face. "What about Celeste?"

Charlotte took a deep breath, bracing herself for the impact of what she was about to say. "Celeste isn't just working with Victor Reynard. They're together. Romantically."

The room fell into a stunned silence. Carter's eyes widened in shock, his face pale as he tried to absorb the weight of Charlotte's words. His daughter—the one he had raised, the one he had trusted—was in a relationship with his sworn enemy?

"That's impossible," Carter said, shaking his head in disbelief. "Celeste wouldn't... she couldn't..."

"She is," Charlotte said firmly. "I've seen it with my own eyes. This isn't just about business, Carter. Celeste and Victor are planning something far more dangerous. And if you don't act soon, you're going to lose everything."

Carter stood frozen, the enormity of the situation pressing down on him like a weight he couldn't bear. The walls were closing in, and the people he had trusted most—his wife, his daughter—had betrayed him in ways he never could have imagined.

He turned back to Charlotte, his voice barely above a whisper. "What do I do?"

Charlotte stepped forward, her eyes meeting his with a steely determination. "We fight. Together."

Carter nodded slowly, knowing deep down that this was the only way forward. The Tomorrow family was on the brink of destruction, but he wasn't ready to let it all fall apart. Not yet.

As they stood together, plotting their next move, the shadows of betrayal loomed large, and the battle for the Tomorrow empire was only just beginning.

# CHAPTER 23

Celeste stepped into the grand foyer of the Tomorrow mansion, her heels clicking against the marble floor with confidence. Her eyes scanned the familiar surroundings, but something was different this time. Sitting in the parlor, attached at her father's hip, was Charlotte. The woman who shouldn't even be in the same country, let alone in their home. A smirk tugged at Charlotte's lips as Celeste locked eyes with her, but Celeste didn't falter. She had expected something like this to happen—just not so soon.

"Celeste," Carter's voice broke through the tension, sounding tired and more weathered than usual. "We need to talk."

Celeste stepped further into the room, straightening her posture. She was not alone, and she needed Carter to remember that. Behind her, Samuel entered, his presence silent but palpable. For a brief moment, she allowed herself to feel reassured. She had Samuel on her side. They had made a deal, after all, and she had managed to keep him close throughout all of this chaos.

Charlotte rose from her seat next to Carter, smoothing out her skirt as she stared at Celeste, eyes gleaming. "It's a little late for talking, don't you think, Carter?"

Celeste clenched her fists at her sides, willing herself to stay composed. "I don't know what you think you're doing here, Charlotte, but you've already lost."

"Lost?" Charlotte tilted her head mockingly. "Oh, I think I've already won."

Before Celeste could respond, Samuel's voice cut through the air.

"She's right, Celeste. I think it's time we put everything out in the open."

Celeste glanced over her shoulder at her brother, a small knot of unease forming in her stomach. Samuel's expression was colder than usual, his posture too relaxed, too calculated. Her heart skipped a beat, but she kept her voice steady. "Sam, we've already discussed this. We're on the same side."

"Are we?" Samuel's voice was dangerously calm as he stepped past her, moving closer to their father. "I don't think we've been on the same side for a long time, Celeste."

The knot in her stomach twisted sharply. This wasn't part of the plan. Her brother—her ally—was turning on her, right here, in front of their father.

"What is this about?" Carter asked, his voice thick with confusion. "Samuel, what are you talking about?"

Celeste opened her mouth to speak, but Charlotte was faster.

"It's about your daughter betraying you, Carter," Charlotte said, her voice dripping with satisfaction. She looked at Celeste, a predator's grin on her lips. "Celeste has been working with Victor Reynard. She's been feeding him secrets, planning your downfall this whole time."

Carter's eyes widened, flickering between his daughter and Charlotte. "That's impossible."

"Oh, it's very possible," Charlotte pressed, taking a step forward. "And if that wasn't enough, your daughter isn't just working with Victor—she's in a relationship with him."

A heavy silence filled the room. Celeste's pulse thundered in her ears, but she kept her expression neutral. This was always going to come out—Charlotte just happened to be the one delivering the final blow. But she wasn't defeated yet.

"I did what I had to do," Celeste said calmly, stepping toward her father. "For the family. For us. Victor was a necessary evil, but I've kept things under control."

"Under control?" Samuel scoffed. "Is that what you call it?"

Celeste turned sharply toward him. "You know why I did this, Sam. You agreed—"

Samuel cut her off, his voice harsh and full of resentment. "I agreed because I needed to know what you were hiding. Now that I do, I see exactly who you are."

Celeste's chest tightened as she realized the trap she'd walked into. Samuel wasn't on her side—he never had been. He had played her, just like she had tried to play him. She had been so focused on manipulating the situation with Victor that she had underestimated her own brother.

Carter, meanwhile, was staring at his daughter as if he didn't know her. "Is this true, Celeste? Have you been working with Reynard?"

She hesitated for the briefest moment. "It was for us, for the family, I told you—"

Carter's voice rose, uncharacteristically sharp. "Answer the question!"

"Yes," she finally admitted, her voice tight. "I've been working with him. But only to keep our enemies close, to protect us."

Charlotte laughed, the sound cold and triumphant. "Protect? You've been plotting against your own family."

Celeste's gaze darted toward the door, her heart racing. Where was Victor? He was supposed to be nearby, waiting for her signal if things went south. He had promised to protect her.

But there was nothing. No sign of him. The knot in her stomach twisted even tighter.

Samuel stepped forward, his voice cutting through her spiraling thoughts. "Victor's not coming, Celeste. You think I didn't know you'd try to pull something like this? You've been sloppy. And now, you're going to pay for it."

Celeste's breath caught in her throat. She looked at her brother, at the smug expression on Charlotte's face, and at the growing rage in her father's eyes. For the first time, she realized she was truly alone.

Her safety, her plan—it had all fallen apart.

"You thought you could play us," Samuel said, his voice low and dangerous. "But you were wrong."

Celeste took a slow step back, her pulse quickening. She had always been the smartest person in the room. She had always been the one with the upper hand. But now, it was all slipping through her fingers.

# CHAPTER 24

The night air was thick with anticipation, the kind that made the hairs on the back of your neck stand up. Evelyn Tomorrow stood just outside the gates of the sprawling mansion, the place that had been her home, her prison, and her battleground. Her face was illuminated by the flicker of the lighter in Victor Reynard's hand, the small flame casting dancing shadows across their faces.

Victor stood beside her, his eyes gleaming with malice and excitement. "Are you sure you're ready for this?" he asked, his voice low, almost a whisper.

Evelyn's eyes never left the mansion. "I've been ready for this for years."

Inside, everything was unraveling just as they had planned. Celeste had played her part well, distracting Carter, Samuel, and Charlotte with her betrayal. The moment Evelyn realized her daughter had aligned with Victor, she hadn't been surprised. It was an opportunity—one she seized without hesitation. Celeste, for all her cunning, had been the perfect pawn. A daughter blinded by her own ambition, believing she was in control, when all along she was just a puppet.

Evelyn knew her children better than they knew themselves. Samuel would never betray his father—Carter had made sure of that. But his loyalty would be his undoing. And Carter, arrogant and blind, always thought he could control the situation. He had no idea that his wife had been plotting his demise for years.

Victor flicked the lighter shut, breaking the silence. "They think they've won," he said, a cruel smile tugging at his lips. "They have no idea what's coming."

Evelyn glanced at him, her expression cold and calculating. "Let them think they've won. It makes the fall that much sweeter."

Inside the mansion, tensions were still high. Celeste could feel her world crumbling beneath her as she stood before her family, exposed and vulnerable for the first time in her life. Samuel's accusations rang in her ears, and Carter's betrayal burned like a hot coal in her chest. Charlotte, with her smug smile, was perched too close to Carter, as though claiming him for herself.

It was all unraveling. But even in her panic, Celeste kept waiting for Victor. She had always trusted that he would appear, that he would save her from the inevitable.

Yet outside, as Victor and Evelyn watched the scene from afar, it became clear that saving Celeste was never part of the plan.

Victor's fingers tightened around the small vial in his pocket. "She's served her purpose."

Evelyn didn't even flinch at the cruelty in his words. She had grown accustomed to it. Celeste had been useful, but now she was just another loose end. And Evelyn had no room for loose ends in the life she envisioned after tonight.

"Do it," she whispered.

Victor gave a nod, his eyes gleaming as he set the small fuse on fire. They watched as the flame crackled and sizzled its way down the line, moving swiftly toward the mansion, toward its inevitable destruction.

Inside, the argument continued to rage, unaware of what was about to befall them. Carter was on his feet, pointing accusingly at Celeste. "I trusted you!" he roared. "How could you do this to me, to us?"

Samuel, however, remained eerily calm. He had gotten what he wanted: the truth. And now, all that was left was to watch Celeste fall apart.

But Celeste's mind was racing. She knew something was wrong. Victor should have appeared by now. He should have—

A sudden, loud crack echoed from outside the mansion. Celeste's head whipped toward the window, her heart leaping into her throat.

"What was that?" Samuel asked, frowning.

Then, the flames came.

It started as a low roar, the crackle of fire quickly turning into a deafening blaze. The windows shattered as flames began to lick the edges of the mansion, spreading with unnatural speed. Smoke poured into the room, curling around them like a deadly serpent.

"What the hell—" Carter started, but the fire was moving too fast.

Celeste's eyes widened as she realized what was happening. This wasn't an accident. This was a plan. And she was caught in the middle of it.

"No!" she screamed, rushing toward the door, but the flames had already consumed the exits.

Samuel grabbed Charlotte, pulling her toward the far side of the room. Carter, too stunned to react at first, finally sprang into action, trying to figure out how to save his family.

Outside, Evelyn and Victor stood back, watching as the mansion was swallowed by flames. The heat from the fire was intense, and Evelyn could feel it on her skin, but she didn't move. She didn't flinch. She only smiled.

"It's done," Victor said, his voice barely audible over the roar of the flames.

Evelyn nodded. "Let them burn."

As the mansion became engulfed, the glow of the fire reflected in her eyes, making her look almost otherworldly. She had won. Carter, Samuel, Charlotte—none of them would survive this. Celeste, her once-ambitious daughter, would perish in the blaze, taking her foolish dreams of power with her.

But even as the flames raged, Evelyn felt no guilt. This was what had to be done. She had waited too long, sacrificed too much, to let sentiment or weakness stop her now.

As the chapter closed, the mansion stood like a beacon of destruction, a pillar of fire lighting up the night. Inside, the lives of Carter, Samuel, Celeste, and Charlotte hung in the balance—each moment a battle for survival as the inferno closed in around them.

And outside, Evelyn and Victor watched, waiting for the final moment when everything they had built came crashing down in flames.

# EPILOGUE

The night sky was alight with flames as the Tomorrow mansion burned, its once-pristine walls crumbling under the inferno's relentless assault. Charlotte stumbled out into the open air, choking on smoke as she gasped for breath. Her face was smeared with soot, and her clothes were singed, but she was alive. Barely.

Behind her, the crackling roar of the fire swallowed everything. Carter's agonized scream echoed from deep within the mansion, a sound that sent a shiver down Charlotte's spine. The man who had built his empire, the man who had tried to control everything—was gone. Burned alive in the flames of his own home.

She turned, looking back at the mansion as the roof caved in with a violent crash. Her hands trembled, not from fear, but from the weight of what had just happened. Samuel was unaccounted for. So was Celeste. She had no way of knowing if they had made it out—or if they were still trapped inside, consumed by the fire. The uncertainty gnawed at her, but she had taken precautions. She wasn't leaving this to chance.

Before the fire, before the chaos, she had ensured that her son—Carter's son—would be named heir. There had been a moment, just days before, when Carter had signed the deed. She had been with him, his trust still lingering despite the mounting tensions. If anything were to happen, if Carter were to fall, his empire would go to his sons. Both of them. Samuel and the son he had unknowingly fathered with Charlotte.

Celeste was written out. Erased from the legacy she had tried so hard to control. A smirk tugged at the corners of Charlotte's lips. For all of Celeste's scheming, she would inherit nothing. Charlotte had seen to that.

But as she stood there, watching the fire devour what was left of the Tomorrow legacy, a shadow moved in the distance. Her smile faded.

From the ruins of the mansion, emerging like a ghost from the flames, was Celeste.

She was wounded—her face streaked with blood, her clothes torn and burned—but she was alive. Barely. And with every step she took toward them, it was clear that something in her had changed. There was no longer fear or desperation in her eyes. There was only cold, steely resolve.

Victor and Evelyn stood waiting near the edge of the property, the blaze illuminating their faces. Victor's eyes gleamed with a mixture of triumph and hunger. Evelyn's face, on the other hand, remained impassive, her cold gaze fixed on her daughter as she approached.

"Carter is dead," Celeste said, her voice hoarse from the smoke and the pain of her injuries. "His reign is over."

Evelyn stepped forward, her lips curling into a smile. "And now it's ours."

Victor nodded, his eyes sweeping over Celeste's battered form. "You made it out. Good. We'll need you for what comes next."

Celeste looked between them, her mother and the man she had once believed was her salvation. The truth of her situation settled over her like a shroud. Her father was dead. Samuel—her brother, her rival—was missing. Perhaps dead, perhaps not. And here, in the ashes of everything she had once fought for, she realized that her war wasn't over.

But before she could speak, a soft sound cut through the air. A quiet, almost mocking clap.

Charlotte stepped out from the shadows, her eyes gleaming with satisfaction. She had been watching the scene unfold, and now she made her presence known.

"You think it's over?" Charlotte's voice rang out, her lips curling into a triumphant smile. "You really think you've won?"

Victor turned, his expression hardening as he eyed Charlotte. "What are you talking about?"

Charlotte's smirk deepened as she met Celeste's gaze. "Carter may be dead, but you're not inheriting anything, Celeste. Your father made sure of that. You're out. Written off the deed. The Tomorrow empire isn't yours. It never will be."

For the first time, Celeste's calm façade cracked. "What?"

"Carter signed the deed," Charlotte said, her voice dripping with satisfaction. "Before the fire, before any of this. His estate, his empire—it goes to his sons. Both of them. Samuel... and the son he had with me."

Evelyn's eyes widened in surprise, a flash of anger crossing her face. Victor, too, stiffened beside her.

"You had a child with Carter?" Evelyn spat, her voice dripping with contempt.

Charlotte smiled wickedly, stepping forward as she relished in the revelation. "Yes. And that child is now the heir to everything Carter owned. The company, the estate, the legacy—all of it. My son is the rightful heir. Not Samuel. Not Celeste. My son."

The weight of Charlotte's words hung in the air like a hammer poised to strike. Celeste's mind reeled. She had been so focused on destroying her father, on taking everything from him, that she hadn't seen this coming. She hadn't anticipated Charlotte's final move.

Victor's hand curled into a fist at his side, his eyes narrowing at Charlotte. "And where is this son of yours?"

Charlotte's smile never wavered. "Safe. Far away from all of this. But when the dust settles, he'll come forward. He'll claim what's rightfully his. And there's nothing any of you can do about it."

For the first time that night, Victor's confidence wavered. Evelyn, too, looked as if the ground had shifted beneath her feet. Celeste stood frozen, her heart pounding in her chest as she realized just how far ahead Charlotte had been playing.

She had been outmaneuvered. Again.

Charlotte took one last look at the burning mansion behind them, then turned her back on the fire, her steps steady as she walked away into the darkness.

"Good luck," she called over her shoulder, her voice thick with triumph. "You're going to need it."

And just like that, she disappeared into the night, leaving Celeste, Victor, and Evelyn to face the ashes of their crumbling empire, unsure of what the future held—and whether they would even survive it.